BENNY'S BARMY BITS

Alexa Tewkesbury

Yo! I'm Benny – and this is my life. It's full of crazy things like annoying teachers and embarrassing parents, not to mention all the top stuff I get up to with my mates in the Topz Gang. Being part of the Gang is ace. If you don't know who we are, you can find out all about us on the next page.

A lot's been happening to me lately and I've really had to learn to trust God. That's something that can be quite hard to do, especially if there's stuff going on that you're scared or worried about. I've also discovered that I'm not always right about everything (shock, horror!). In fact, sometimes I'm so NOT right, I'm off the planet!

That's the weird thing about keeping a diary. The more you write in it, the more you find out about yourself – whether you want to or not! So, if you're after the inside story, get reading.

This is my barmy life – **AND I'M LOVING IT!**

HI! WE'RE THE TOPZ GANG

– Topz because we all live at the 'top' of something …
either in houses at the top of the hill, at the top of the
flats by the park, even sleeping in a top bunk counts!
We are all Christians, and we go to Holly Hill School.

We love Jesus, and try to work out our faith in God
in everything we do – at home, at school and with our
friends. That even means trying to show God's love to
the Dixons Gang who tend to be bullies, and can be a
real pain!

If you'd like to know more about us, visit our website
at **www.cwr.org.uk/topz**. You can read all about us,
and how you can get to know and understand the Bible
more by reading our 'Topz' notes, which are great fun,
and written every two months just for you!

WEDNESDAY 13TH MAY

Homework: Learn spelling list
To do: Phone Greg about youth club table tennis tournament/school mag stuff
Mood: Very bad

5.00pm

Why oh why did we have to end up with Mr Mallory as our class teacher this term? He is SO annoying! I know we've only got him while Mrs Francis is off having her baby, but of all the teachers in the whole, entire universe, why did we have to end up with him?!

Whenever he asks a question, almost the whole class can have their hands up to answer it, but if my hand is DOWN he <u>still</u> asks me. Then when I don't know the answer (which I'm obviously not going to otherwise I would have put my hand UP – duh) he sighs and says things like, 'Oh dearie me, is there any life at all on Planet Benny today?' And if he asks something I <u>do</u> know the answer to, I stick my hand straight up and he totally ignores me!

He's also got this thing about my fringe. I'm sick of him making pathetic comments like, 'What's the weather like under there?' and 'What a relief, Benny. For a dreadful minute I thought you'd been eaten by your hair.'

Does he really think he's funny? My toothbrush could make better jokes than he does. And what I want to know is WHAT'S MY HAIR GOT TO DO WITH HIM ANYWAY??

Danny says maybe he's jealous of me.

I said, 'Why would Mr Mallory be jealous of me?'

He said, 'In case you haven't noticed, he's bald.'

I said, 'Well, that's not <u>my</u> fault. Anyway, you can't pick on someone just because they've got hair and you haven't.'

Then John said, 'You know what the perfect solution is, don't you?'

I said, 'No, what?'

He said, 'You could shave your head.'

Great. It's always good to know you can rely on your friends to sort out your problems.

6.00pm

Just spoken to Greg about the table tennis on Friday. He's put Josie and Dave on my team – mega cool, we can't lose!

I moaned on about Mr Mallory again and Greg says I've got to give him a chance. (I suppose he would say that. He's a grown-up. They always stick together.) He said it can't be easy taking over someone else's class just for a term and, believe it or not, the guy's probably quite nervous.

<u>He's</u> nervous? What about me? I never know what he's going to come out with next. All I know is it WON'T be funny.

'Just try and do your best for him,' Greg said. 'He can't ask for more than that.' Then he told me to go and practise my backhand for Friday.

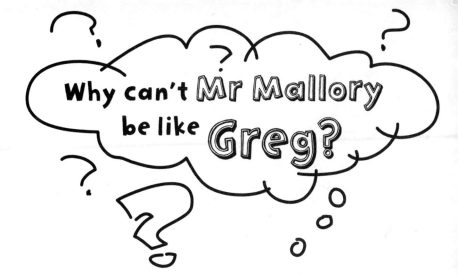

Later

Been through the questionnaires I've had back and all I can say is – WHAT IS THE POINT?

Apparently voting day for the new editor of the school mag is going to be the first day back after half term so, if you want to be voted for, you have to get your advertising poster finished and up on the board by next Monday. I've written all about myself and why I'd be the best person to be editor. I've even put a photo in so the little kids will know who I am if they want to vote for me, and it all looks really cool. All I've got left to do is my plan for what the mag will include if I get voted in.

Dad says the best magazines are the ones full of things you really want to read.

Brilliant, I thought. So I made up a questionnaire to try and find out what everyone at school was interested in. I asked things like: What's your favourite sport? Would you like a jokes page? Should we run competitions? Any suggestions?

I'm going to have to scrap it though. I've had loads of answers like, 'Hate sport', 'Do you actually know any funny jokes?', 'Competitions are only worth doing if the prizes are good', and most of the suggestions for what to include are things like horse riding, hair and fashion and a problem page!

I said to Dad, 'How on earth am I supposed to make a magazine out of that?'

Dad said, 'The trouble is, if you don't give people what they want, they won't vote for you.'

I said, 'But Dad, how am I supposed to write a problem page?'

He said, 'Mmm. It's a problem.'

Very funny. (Not.)

8.00pm

There is no way I'm doing a magazine with a problem page.

What is this fascination with other people's problems anyway?

I'm not doing hair and fashion either.

Actually, I don't think I can be bothered. If they want a soppy old-fashioned mag, they can have one. I never wanted to be the editor in the first place.

Stupid mag.

8.20pm

Who cares what other people want? This is MY mag and I'm having a car page, a footie page, a 'my favourite crisps' page, crosswords, wordsearches, jokes and loads of competitions. I might have a letters page – but only interesting letters about skateboarding and stuff. Not problems. It's going to be so ace! They'd all have to be mad to vote for anyone else.

And when I'm editor, Mr Mallory will have to admit that I AM good at something.

8.30pm

 Uh oh. Forgot to learn spellings. Have to get up early.

THURSDAY 14TH MAY

Homework: Maths sheet
To do: Clean trainers for tournament tomorrow
Mood: Worse than yesterday (yes, that is possible) – details coming up …

grrrrr

5.30pm
Rubbish, rubbish, RUBBISH day!

Rubbish thing number 1:

Mr Mallory did the spelling test like a quiz but he wouldn't let us write the words down. We had to spell them out loud. I can't do it like that. I need to write them down. I'm sure Mr Mallory knows that. He just enjoys making me look like a total loser – which I did because I got all my words wrong, and Danny and Rebecca aren't good spellers either so our team came last.

Rubbish thing number 2:

Put my school mag poster up.

Mr Mallory looked at it and said, 'So, Benny, you'd like to be the new editor, would you?'

I thought, no, that's why I've done a poster. (How did this man get to be a teacher anyway?)

I said, 'Yes. I think I'd do a really good job.'

He said, 'You know what every good school magazine should have?'

I said, 'No.'

He said, 'An editor who can see out from under his hair.'

Rubbish thing number 3:

Played football at lunchtime and guess who fell and sprained his wrist so he won't be able to be in the table tennis tomorrow? Dave! His mum had to come and take him to casualty. I should have known it was too good to be true when Greg put him on my team.

I said to Josie, 'Of course, you know he's ruined everything. Without him on our side we'll never win.'

But she just said I was being selfish. She said that Dave had really hurt himself and I should be worrying about <u>him</u> and not about how it affected me.

It was like talking to my mum. Scary!

Doesn't she realise this is THE tournament we're about to play? It's not just any old competition. Girls just don't have that 'need to win' thing. Now Greg'll probably end up putting Paul on our team. Paul's great and everything, just not at table tennis. We really needed Dave.

Rubbish thing number 4:

Just spoken to Greg. Yup, we've got Paul. Whoop-de-doo.

(oop, sorry Paul!)

9.15pm

Can't sleep. Sometimes it feels as if the whole universe is ganging up on me. I said that to Dad but he said no matter how we feel, God's always on our side.

He said, 'You have to say, "Okay, Lord, so things aren't going well, but I know you're still in charge."'

I said, 'I don't feel as if <u>anyone's</u> in charge at the moment.'

He said I had to try and look at everything more positively – eg:

1. Although he's annoying, at least Mr Mallory is only around for this term.
2. I've got just as much chance as anyone else of being voted in as editor of the school mag.
3. At least I'm not the one with the bad wrist so I can still play in the tournament.

Then he said, 'Winning the table tennis tournament would be fantastic, but if you don't, so what? The important thing is to have fun joining in.'

Have you noticed how, in situations like this, grown-ups just can't help going on about the joining in thing?

I said, 'Dad, how can losing be fun?'

He said, 'Look, God doesn't want you to be miserable. He wants you to enjoy yourself. And He wants to be the most important part of your life. More important than some tournament. Talk to Him. I'm sure you'll feel better when you do and then you'll get a good night's sleep.'

9.45pm

Why is praying always so hard when you're grumpy?

I've done it, though.

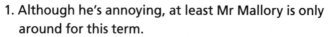

12

I said, 'Dear Lord, please help me to remember that you <u>are</u> in charge of my life and that you want the best for me. And I'm sorry for being mean about Dave's wrist. After all, it's not his fault and he's probably disappointed he can't play in the tournament too. Plus it must have really hurt. His lips went sort of blue.'

(Only just remembered that. Ouch.)

Then I asked for tomorrow to go a bit better.

I think I feel like going to sleep now.

(I really love my dad, but why does he have to be right all the time?!)

9.50pm

Just had a really positive thought about Mr Mallory. Maybe he's actually an alien from another planet, and in the night a massive spaceship will land in his front garden with all its lights flashing and a little green man will knock on his door and tell him it's time to go back to where he came from.

You see, Dad, I AM trying. I mean, how positive is that?

If Mr Mallory did get carried away into outer space, I wonder if I'd end up missing him because, all of a sudden, he just wasn't here any more …

Let me think …

Dum de dum …

NO.

FRIDAY 15TH MAY

Homework: Science (revision)/Spellings (urrgh!)
To do: Win the tournament, otherwise please let there be nothing (except trainers)
Mood: Improving

4.30pm

Better day so far. Hung around near the laptops for a bit (where the school mag editor posters are up) to see if anyone stopped to read mine. Quite a few did but I had to make out I didn't notice. I pretended to be looking at a PowerPoint demo about tadpoles.

Dave was at school with his wrist all bandaged up and I said sorry I'd been off with him when he hurt himself. He was cool about it though and said he'd have felt the same if it had been me. He's going to come down later and cheer us on.

Also, NO MR MALLORY! (No, the aliens didn't get him, it's just I'd forgotten we were having a drum workshop day so I only had to be trapped in the classroom with him for registration.)

WOW!

These people came into school (they had a mega cool truck with paintings down the side of drums with flames shooting out of them where they were being hit by drumsticks) and we were doing all sorts of stuff about beats and rhythms. There were loads of different drums to have a go on. Dave could only use his left hand but he said it was fine – a bit like playing darts wearing an eye patch … I always knew he was a nutter.

Mr Mallory was loitering in the background, but he didn't get the chance to make any dumb comments like, 'Hang on to your hats, everybody, I think Benny's coming out for air.' I wanted to imagine my drum was actually his bald head – but I didn't suppose Dad would think that was a 'positive' thought, so I tried not to. (It was hard, though.)

Forgot to clean trainers yesterday. Better go and do it now. Mum says. I asked her why it mattered. I mean, after all, this is a table tennis tournament we're talking about, not a who's got the cleanest trainers in Holly Hill tournament, but she just said not to be cheeky – as if!

5.30pm

Tournament starts in an hour. Just done twenty press-ups (well, six) as a warm-up. They're supposed to be great for upper-body strength. Actually they just hurt.

I thought I could ask God to let us win, but I suppose that's not a very good prayer. After all, it's not His job to make anyone win or lose. So instead I said, 'Please, Lord God, help us all to be the best we can be and to be happy with the result, whatever it is.'

I can't imagine being happy if we lose but Greg always says don't think about things too much, just give them to God.

(My arms are killing me.)

SATURDAY 16TH MAY
Homework: As above
To do: Homework
Mood: Fanstonkingtastic!

8.00am

WE ARE THE CHAMPIONS, THE CHAMPIONS, THE CHAMPIONS!!

Well, we're not exactly the champions – we came second, but I never thought we'd do that well. Paul was magic! His wrist action's not great but his footwork's dead nifty. I felt really guilty for not wanting him on the team.

So I said, 'Paul, you're MESMERISING. I hope we're on the same side in the winter play-offs.'

I still felt a bit bad though so I thought I'd better say

sorry for thinking he'd be useless when he obviously wasn't at all.

He said, 'I didn't know you thought I'd be useless.'

I said, 'Oh. Right.'

He said, 'Anyway, forget it. I usually am useless.'

Then we had a chip fight, which was going really well until one got Greg in the back of the neck and he told us to pack it in and clean up – not easy as half the chips had got squished onto shoes so most of the floor was looking a bit of a wreck. Whoops.

Just realised God answered my prayer! We didn't win but it's cool. In fact, it's better than cool! I never thought not winning could feel even better than winning.

(I think I must have left some squished chip on my trainers. Mum's ranting that she's found something slimy on the carpet. Now she's calling me. Ho hum …)

4.10pm

Definitely need a shower. Been playing Topz rules footie with the Gang and it's burning hot out. Paul actually scored two goals. Paul NEVER scores a goal. Well, hardly ever. What is going on here?

Something else weird. Sarah says she saw the Dixons Gang messing about on the swings earlier and she's dead certain Mickey Martin was with them. He couldn't have been though, he's in Australia. The whole family moved out there last year. It's just about the right distance away too. Mickey Martin was seriously not nice to me.

I told Sarah she must need her eyes testing. It couldn't have been him.

It really could not have been him.

7.30pm

Told Mum all about the Topz rules game this afternoon. She says I ought to be a sports journalist.

If you're a sports journalist, does that mean you can cover every single sport?

What a fanstonkingtastic job!

How old do you have to be? Can I start now?

9.00pm

Can't wait till I'm editor of the school mag.

TUESDAY 19TH MAY

Homework: Read Chapter 3 of 'Treasure Island'
To do: Is there any point in doing anything?
Mood: Why me, oh why me, oh WHY ME?

4.45pm

It's not fair! It wasn't fair the last time it happened so it's even less fair this time because now we know how totally and agonisingly DEADLY it's going to be!

I said, 'Mum, you cannot be serious.'

She said, 'I am. Auntie Janice and little Jacob want to come and stay next week and I said it'd be lovely to see them. What's the problem? It's only for a few days.'

A few days?! Like, four!

I said, 'You're talking about Monday to Thursday. Next week is half term. I'm going to need my space.'

She said, 'You'll have plenty of space in the spare room. I'm sorry they have to be in yours again, but there are two of them and they're going to need your bunk bed.'

I said, 'Mum, don't you remember what happened to my Scalextric the last time they were here? Jake decided

to use the fish tank as a car wash.'

She said, 'Yes, well, he <u>was</u> only three.'

(I'm sorry, but what has age got to do with it?)

I said, 'What about all the slimy lumps of half-chewed sandwich you found in the washing machine the day they went home? What a waste of a sandwich. And the plastic cup he must have stuck in the oven that you only discovered was there when you were cooking my birthday cake? Don't you remember that revolting smell? The kitchen stank for weeks!'

I wasn't being unkind, but sometimes grown-ups need reminding about these things.

Mum obviously didn't think so.

She said, 'Don't be like that. Auntie Janice has had a difficult time lately. She just wants a bit of a break somewhere else.'

I said, 'Fine. But why does the somewhere else have to be here?'

Mum said, 'Because she's my sister, Benjamin, and I want to see her.'

Benjamin

That was it, then. Subject closed. You don't mess with Mum once she starts calling you 'Benjamin'.

I'm not giving up, though. I've still got my secret weapon. Dad. Jake ripped up his 'Favourite Walks Through The British Isles' book last time. Dad won't want them here either.

7.30pm

Dad got home.

I waited till Mum had gone out to the kitchen, then I said, 'Dad, I really need to talk to you.'

He said, 'Let me get my shoes off first.'

'Dad,' I said, 'believe me, what I've got to say you're going to want to hear with your shoes on.'

He said, 'What are you talking about?'

I pushed the lounge door closed and whispered, 'The nightmare's about to begin again.'

He just looked at me.

I said, 'Jake.'

He still just looked at me.

I said, 'Auntie Janice and Jake.'

He looked as if he might be going to say something, but didn't.

I said, 'They're coming to
stay. Here. In our house. Next
week.'

He said, 'I know.'

'What?'

'I know.'

I said, 'How could you
possibly know?'

He said, 'Mum rang
earlier to ask if it was all
right and I said, yes, fine.'

'You said what?' I said.
(It's amazing I could talk at
all.)

'I said, yes, fine,' he said. 'Is it all
right if I take my shoes off now?'

8.00pm
I'm speechless.
Wordless.
I have no words.

8.45pm
How can they do this to me?

9.00pm
They just said goodnight.
I didn't answer.
I have no words.

9.30pm
IT'S ALL SO UNFAIR!

WEDNESDAY 20TH MAY
Homework: Who cares?
To do: Who cares?
Mood: I haven't got one. I'm moodless

5.00pm

That's it, then. Half term's blitzed. I was going to spend all week putting together some special pages for the school mag. As soon as I'm editor, I wanted to be able to get a copy out really quickly – a sort of introductory one. And I thought I'd watch some football or motor racing or something on TV and do practice write-ups so that when I start being a sports journalist I'll be really good at it.

How can I possibly do any of that now? There'll be no peace. It'll be endless 'Thomas the Tank Engine' on the DVD player (not that I've anything against 'Thomas the Tank Engine', but fifty million times a day?), and that other stupid thing Jake watched over and over again last time till it got so buried in my head that I actually found myself singing one of the songs in the middle of Sainsbury's. Out loud. Next to the frozen pizzas. Unbelievable.

Doesn't Auntie Janice know that too much TV rots your brain?

Not only that, but everything in this house will be sticky.

5.30pm

Paul helped me get the rounders bats out at lunchtime. He wanted to know what was wrong.

I said, 'Nothing. If you don't mind being kicked out of your own bedroom so it can be trashed by your small, four-year-old cousin who likes eating toothpaste and dribbling it back out in disgusting great dollops all over your chess set.'

Paul said, 'I didn't know you played chess.'

I said, 'As far as my parents are concerned, my feelings count for nothing.'

Paul said, 'I had a chess set once. I lost one of the bishops.'

I MEAN,
WHAT IS THE POINT??

THURSDAY 21ST MAY

Homework: Colour in map
To do: Enjoy spending last few precious days in my un-trashed bedroom
Mood: Apparently nobody cares

5.30pm

Can't think of anything to write. So that's what I'm going to write – nothing.

FRIDAY 22ND MAY

Homework: Revise times tables
To do: Try and ignore Mum and
Dad without them realising I'm
ignoring them
Mood: Desperate

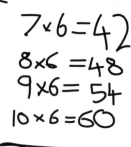

$7 \times 6 = 42$
$8 \times 6 = 48$
$9 \times 6 = 54$
$10 \times 6 = 60$

5.00pm

This morning Dad said, 'Isn't it about time we had a chat about this?'

He'd just made me some toast so I had to say thank you.

He said, 'Benny, you know you're being very childish.'

So? I'm a child, aren't I? What else am I going to be?

He said, 'How are we going to sort this out? You can't just refuse to talk to us for the rest of your life.'

Bother. He'd noticed. I was trying not to make it too obvious.

He said, 'Sometimes we have to do things, not because we particularly want to, but because it's kind to other people. Uncle Phil's been working in America for the last six months. He doesn't get home that often. It's not easy for Auntie Janice managing on her own with Jacob.'

It wouldn't be easy for an entire army to manage with Jacob.

He went on, 'She just wants to get away for a few days.'

Then he stopped. He was looking at me. I knew this was where I was supposed to say something. How could I get out of it?

I had a brainwave. Don't talk with your mouthful. Grown-ups are always saying that. I grabbed the last

piece of toast and shoved most of it in my mouth. (A bit less might have been good. I could hardly chew, let alone talk.)

Dad carried on looking at me. Then he did one of his meaningful sighs.

'Fine,' he said and went to finish getting ready for work.

Mum came into the kitchen and looked at me too. I hoped she wouldn't say anything.

She didn't.

5.20pm

Greg just rang. Youth club bowling trip this evening is cancelled. We're going next week instead.

Greg said, 'I see you're talking to <u>me</u>, then.'

I said, 'Why wouldn't I be?'

He said, 'Your mum just told me you've hardly said a word to her all week.'

Thanks, Mum, I thought.

Greg said, 'We're not going bowling after all, so youth club will be in the church hall, usual time. Are you coming?'

'Yeah, of course,' I said.

He said, 'Great, see you there. And if you need a chat, just come and tell me.'

She's told him. Mum's told him everything. She must have done.

I don't need a chat. I just need my half term back.

9.00pm
I have a really bad feeling I may have got this all wrong.

SATURDAY 23RD MAY
Homework: None (half term)
To do: Not sure
Mood: Not sure

7.30am
Yes, it's half past seven in the morning and I'm writing already. This is SO not like me.

I was playing table tennis with Paul, John and Danny at youth club. (Paul must have been having a good run last week. He was back to his usual form yesterday – useless.)

Then Greg came over and gave me a bit of paper. He'd written a Bible reference on it.

'Have a look at that when you get home,' he said. 'It might help you sort things out.'

I wasn't going to bother. I mean, how could a Bible reference help sort out the unavoidable arrival (well, I could have avoided it, but Mum and Dad apparently can't) of my sticky, dribbly baby cousin? How could a Bible reference sort out the fact that my parents haven't even begun to understand what this is going to be like for me? How could a Bible reference sort out anything this desperate?

I stuck the bit of paper in my drawer and went to bed.

Then I decided I'd look at it anyway. So I got up again.

Greg had written down John 13 v 34. I got my Bible, found the verse and read it.

I have seriously got this all wrong.

9.00am

Had breakfast with Mum and Dad. Didn't know what to say.

9.30am

Why is it so hard to talk to people you've been trying not to talk to?

10.00am

Paul rang.

He said, 'Have you cheered up yet?'

I said, 'What would you do if you needed to say sorry but you felt a bit of a geek doing it?'

He said, 'I'm used to feeling a bit of a geek. I'd probably just say sorry anyway.'

I said, 'Even if it was really hard?'

He said, 'Yeah. But if it was that hard I think I'd ask God to help me out. Some things are just too tough on your own. That's what Greg always says.'

I said, 'Thanks, Paul.'

He said, 'Anything to get you to lighten up. So – who have you got to say sorry to?'

'Bye, Paul,' I said.

11.30am

Mum knocked on the door and asked if I wanted a chocolate-banana milkshake because she'd just made one.

I thought, this could be the moment. Go for it. Say yes.

So I said, 'Yes. Please.'

Mum said, 'Are you coming down?'

Oh great, I thought. If I say no that'll be as good as saying, 'Forget it, I'm still not talking to you', but if I say yes then I'll have to face them and say sorry now. And I'll end up looking like a complete idiot.

'Are you coming down, Benny?' she said again.

At least I'm not 'Benjamin' today.

'I'll be there in a minute,' I said.

I grabbed my Bible and looked at that verse from Greg again. It's something Jesus said:

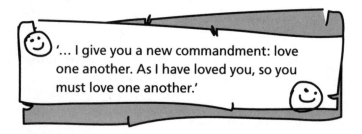

'... I give you a new commandment: love one another. As I have loved you, so you must love one another.'

Then I thought about what Paul said on the phone – some things are just too tough on your own. And I prayed like mad.

I said something like, 'Lord Jesus, I'm so sorry. I've been so NOT loving. It's not Jake's fault he's only four. He can't help doing mega annoying stuff and being really disgusting. I mean if you can't be a pain when you're four years old, when can you be? And I've been horrible to Mum and Dad. They're trying to be kind and all I've done is wind them up. I'm sorry. I'm really, really sorry. I've got to go and talk to them now. I've got to tell them I'm sorry too – and I don't know how to do it. Please, please, please help me. I can't do this on my own.'

When I got downstairs Mum was in the living room reading her magazine.

I said, 'Where's Dad?'

She said, 'He's just popped out to the shops. He won't be long.'

Brilliant, I thought, I'm going to have to say sorry twice – once to her now and once to Dad when he gets back.

Not only that but Mum was acting SO normal. Hadn't she noticed that I was suddenly sort of speaking to her again after three days of almost nothing?

I said, 'Mum.'

She said, 'Your milkshake's in the kitchen.'

I said, 'Can I talk to you?'

She said, 'If you want.'

'I do want,' I said. 'I want … I want …'

She put down her magazine.

'What is it you want, Benny?'

'I'm … sorry.'

She reached out and gave my hand a big squeeze.

'It's all right, darling,' she said. 'I know it was a bit difficult with Jacob last time, and I know it's not easy trying to be kind to people when you don't feel like it. Especially when it means you've really got to put yourself out. I do understand. You think I don't, but I do.'

'Yeah,' I said, 'I'm really sorry. That's all.'

She said, 'I know you are. It's just that Auntie Janice and Jacob need lots of love at the moment. So that's what we've got to give them.'

'Like Jesus says to do,' I said.

'Yeah,' she said. 'Like Jesus says to do.'

5.00pm

Been playing footie with Dad in the park. He's not that bad. For an old person.

Glad all that saying sorry bit's out of the way. I suppose it wasn't so hard after all. In the end.

Actually, it was. Well, not hard, exactly, just … you know … difficult.

Anyway, it's no fun not talking to people. You've got no way to test your jokes out.

9.00pm

Dad came in to say goodnight.
I said, 'Dad, do you still love me?'
He said, 'Of course I still love you, you lemon.'

30

SUNDAY 24TH MAY

Homework: Still none
To do: Move into spare room
Mood: OK – sort of-ish. I suppose

2.00pm

At Sunday Club Paul said, 'Did you do it?'

I said, 'What?'

He said, 'Say sorry.'

I said, 'Oh, that. Yes I did.'

He said, 'How was it?'

I said, 'All right.'

He asked if I wanted to go over this afternoon and watch the football at his house, but I had to say no. We're sorting out my bedroom because Auntie Janice and Jake are arriving tomorrow. Mum says that, after last time, it's probably sensible to move a few things out of the way, just in case Jake should still turn out to be a bit of a wrecker. Although apparently Auntie Janice has promised to keep more of an eye on him this time.

Paul said he'd think of me while he was lounging on the sofa with his dad eating crisps.

'Thanks,' I said.

It's hard to see Jake as a 'bit of a wrecker'. He's more like a one-toddler disaster zone.

And he's about to hit my bedroom.

Grunt.

8.30pm

I'm sitting in a cupboard. It's not really a cupboard, it's our spare room, but it's as small as a medium-sized cupboard. It's also very pink. Mum says it's not, it's 'wild heather', but basically it's pink.

There's a bed jammed against a chest of drawers, and some other stuff that Mum never seems to know what to do with. And I've just about managed to cram my Scalextric, some of my books and my CD player in as well.

I'm going to sleep in here tonight. Mum says I don't have to but I thought I may as well.

I said, 'Maybe they'll go out a lot.'

She said, 'Maybe we can all go out together.'

I said, 'Yeah,' not very enthusiastically.

Oh help. I wonder if loving everyone, especially the people you don't feel like loving, is the hardest thing God wants us to do.

MONDAY 25TH MAY

To do: Keep asking God to help me love Jake
Mood: Definitely not loving at the moment

10.00am
Woke up and couldn't remember where I was. Then it came back to me. I'd gone to sleep in a pink cupboard.

11.00am

They'll be here soon.

11.15am

I still don't want them to come.

I've prayed three times today already, 'Lord, please help me not to feel like this.' Nothing's changed, though. I STILL don't want them to come.

11.45am
They're here.
Half term just died.

HALF TERM RIP

9.00pm

I think it's going to be all right. I can't believe it, but I really think it is. In fact, it could even be quite cool. Jake's still a bit sticky and all over the place, but so far he hasn't wrecked anything. AND Auntie Janice has given me a radio-controlled car.

'Open it later, though,' she said. 'The last thing we want is Jake clapping eyes on it.'

When it was Jake's bedtime he asked me, 'Where are you sleeping?'

I said, 'I'm in the spare room.'

He said, 'I want to be in the spare room too.'

I said, 'Sorry, you can't. There's only one bed.'

He said, 'But I only need one bed.'

I said, 'Yeah, but then where am I going to sleep? Anyway, you get to sleep in my bunk and bunk beds are really wicked.'

Jake thought for a minute, then he said, 'I want you to read me my story.'

No one's ever asked me to read them a story before. Except at school. And teachers only ask you to read so they can interrupt and tell you what words you're getting wrong. Especially Mr Mallory.

Auntie Janice started to say, 'Oh, come on, Jakey, I'm not sure Benny feels like reading at the moment,' but suddenly, this mega weird thing happened.

I said, 'No, that's all right, I don't mind reading to him.'

I honestly said that!

Partly it was weird because I said it, but what was even more weird was that I meant it. I really didn't mind reading to him.

Auntie Janice said, 'Are you sure? He's probably going to want "The Gingerbread Man" – several times.'

I said it was fine and it was sort of nice to be asked.

Jake did want 'The Gingerbread Man' – more than several times. I'd probably still be reading it to him now if Auntie Janice hadn't come in and said, 'All right, Jacob, I think that's enough gingerbread men for one night, don't you?'

Then Jake said he really liked having a big boy for a cousin.

Weirder and weirder. I really like him too. And he likes my reading.

Maybe I need to rethink this whole thing about being a sports journalist.

9.30pm

Dad came into my cupboard to say goodnight.

I said, 'Dad, I think I could be wrong about wanting to be a sports journalist. I think maybe I ought to be a teacher.'

Dad said, 'What makes you think that?'

I said, 'Jake really likes me.'

Dad said, 'I thought having Jacob here was going to be the worst thing in the history of the world's worst things?'

I said, 'So did I. Do you think that happens a lot? You're sure something's going to be mega bad news, but when it actually happens it's a lot better than you thought it was going to be?'

'I expect that depends on what the something is,' Dad said. 'But what we shouldn't do is spend our time worrying. Worry doesn't change a thing. It just puts us in a bad mood.'

I said, 'But if you're a worrying sort of person, it's really hard not to worry.'

Dad said, 'I know. That's why God wants us to give our worries to Him. It doesn't matter how big or how small they are, He just wants to take them away. He wants you to know that He's always there, ready to take care of you.'

I said, 'I think God's been helping me love Jake.'

Dad said, 'Good. And I'm really pleased you're both getting on. But it's probably a bit soon to be making plans to be a teacher.'

I said, 'Do you think so? Maybe I should see how it goes for the rest of the week.'

'Great idea,' Dad said.

9.45pm
Still think I'd make a cool teacher. I'd do sport all day and never give homework.

TUESDAY 26TH MAY

To do: Read Jake 'The Gingerbread Man'
Mood: Good (in an 'I got woken up incredibly early this morning' sort of way)

8.30am

IMPORTANT NOTE TO MYSELF:
Never forget how Jake bounced on you at five o'clock this morning asking for 'The Gingerbread Man' and saying, 'I want my Marmite now.' Are all little kids like this or is it just Jake? Must investigate. Maybe I need to rethink this whole thing about being a teacher. (Jake's just wiped Marmite all down the back of my t-shirt … Now he's licking it off. Nice.)

10.00am

Auntie Janice just said, 'Let's go to the zoo. Jakey loves the animals, don't you Jakey?'

Jake said, 'I want to be an elephant,' and he did that trunk thing where you hold your arm up to your nose and wave it about. Unfortunately he waved it about near an almost full, open bottle of orange, which went flying. The floor wasn't too flooded, though, because Mum happened to be right next to the bottle at the time and a lot of the juice got soaked up in her jeans and ran into her slippers.

Auntie Janice kept saying, 'I am SO sorry,' but Mum said it was fine and maybe going out was a much better idea than staying indoors – there's more space at the zoo.

I said, 'Oh well, it could have been worse. It could have gone all over me.'

Mum didn't say anything. She just squelched off to get changed.

6.00pm

Zoo was cool. John and Sarah were there. We went off and got an ice cream.

Sarah said, 'How's it going with Jake?'

I said, 'Great. It's quite good fun.'

John said, 'How's that then?'

I said, 'I think having Jake to stay could be going to change the entire course of my life.'

John said, 'How's that then?'

I said, 'Do you think I'd make a good teacher?'

Sarah said, 'Why would you want to be a teacher?'

I said, 'I think I might be quite good at it.'

John said, 'How's that then?'

I said, 'John, is that all you can say? – "How's that then?"'

John said, 'How do you mean?'

Sarah poked him on the nose with her Cornetto (which probably made a bit more of a splodge than she thought it was going to).

When we got to the elephants, Jake showed them his elephant impression. They didn't take much notice.

Jake said, 'Look, elephants. I'm an elephant too.'

They still didn't take much notice.

He jumped up and down, waggling his arm in front of his nose and kept saying, 'Look! I'm an elephant too. I'm an elephant too.'

All that happened was one of them turned round and went inside the shelter. Jake looked really upset.

I felt a bit sorry for him so I said, 'Hey, Jakey. I'll be an elephant,' and we both ran off waving our arms up and down trunkily.

That's when I bumped into John and Sarah again.

I said, 'Oh. Hi.'

Sarah said, 'What's with all the arm waving stuff?'

I said, 'We were just being elephants.'

Sarah said, 'I'd never have guessed.'

'Yeah,' I said, 'you know, with trunks and stuff.'

John said, 'How's that then?'

8.45pm

I think I'm getting to like it in my cupboard. It's quite good because I can just about reach everything without having to get off the bed.

Mum squeezed in and said, 'Thanks for playing with Jacob. You're doing a really good job with him.'

I said, 'That's OK. He's all right.'

She said, 'He's a handful though, isn't he?'

'Yes,' I said, 'but, doesn't that make him sort of loveable?'

She said, 'I'm sure it does. In small bursts. I love him to bits.'

I said, 'If God helps you to love someone you thought you weren't even going to like, so you start being nice to them and stuff, do you suppose that person becomes more loveable – because they're being loved?'

Mum said, 'Well, it must make a difference. Knowing you're loved is a good feeling, and if you feel good about yourself that probably makes you easier to get along with.'

'When you love someone, you start to see the good things about them, don't you?' I said. 'I didn't love Jake last time he was here and I couldn't see anything good about him. He was a total nightmare.'

'Mmm,' Mum said. 'This time he's just a bad dream.'

I'm going to say thank You to God. Thanks for helping me love Jake. I mean, God must think <u>I'm</u> a bit of a bad dream a lot of the time, but He still loves me.

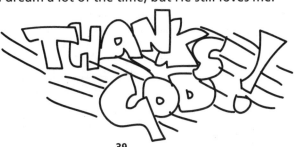

39

WEDNESDAY 27TH MAY

To do: For and against list for being a teacher/for and against list for being a sports journalist
Mood: Yo yo yoh!

3.00pm

We've been doing drumming in the kitchen (Jake and me). Mum's not happy. Jake thought it was great though. We were really clever. We lined up all Mum's saucepans (plus a bucket, but the sound was a bit dead compared to the saucepans), turned them upside down on the floor and hit them with wooden spoons.

Mum said, 'Benny, you're supposed to be setting a good example.'

I said, 'I am. I'm showing Jake there are other things you can do with saucepans than just cook in them.'

Auntie Janice said, 'Jake, don't think this means you can start drumming on my saucepans at home.'

I said, 'No, don't say that. He's learning to be creative.'

Mum said, 'He's learning to make a racket.'

Then Mum made me wash the saucepans. She said it was unhygienic to put anything to do with food on the floor and I ought to know better.

I said, 'Here I am providing ace little kid entertainment and this is the thanks I get.'

There's just no pleasing some grown-ups.

GOOD REASONS TO BE A TEACHER:

I'd get to muck about with little kids.

I could help them feel good about themselves by showing I loved them.

I could read books like 'The Gingerbread Man' without my friends thinking there must be something seriously wrong with me.

GOOD REASONS TO BE A SPORTS JOURNALIST:

I could watch as much sport as I want to all week because it's my job.

I could watch sport at the weekends, too, because everyone needs time off.

People would think I was cool.

REASONS NOT TO BE A TEACHER:

Uncool (eg Mr Mallory).

Teachers often wear really bad clothes.

Is it possible to feel loving every single day of term?

REASONS NOT TO BE A SPORTS JOURNALIST:

I might make a better teacher.

Ugh. None of that's very helpful. How am I supposed to decide? It's really hard having to make choices.

41

6.30pm

Nope. Haven't a clue. Still, sometimes there are more important things in life than decisions. Off to watch 'Thomas the Tank Engine'.

8.30pm

Last night in my cupboard. For some reason I feel a bit sad. I mean, why would anyone feel sad about their last night in a pink cupboard – especially when tomorrow night they'll be back in their own room in their own bed surrounded by all their own stuff, with nothing pink in sight?

9.00pm

Danny rang. He said sorry it was late but he'd been worrying about whether to phone me or not. He thought he wouldn't but then he changed his mind because he said I'd find out sooner or later anyway.

'Find out what?' I said.

'About Mickey Martin. You remember the other day when Josie said she saw him in the park?'

Actually, I'd pretty well forgotten.

Danny said, 'Well, she was right. She did see him.'

'So, what does that mean?' I said. 'Is he just here for a visit?'

'No,' Danny said. 'He's back. Apparently his dad didn't like it in Australia. They're back here for good.'

9.15pm

I'm not going to panic. What would be the point?

Mickey Martin might have moved back here but that doesn't mean he'll be coming to Holly Hill School again. And even if he does, just because he had it in for me before he went away doesn't mean he still will.

Anyway all the bullying stuff was sorted out. It wouldn't start up again. It couldn't. I'm not going to be scared of Mickey Martin.

9.30pm
Dad put his head round the door and said, 'Bet you're looking forward to getting your own bed back.'

I said, 'Yeah.'

He said, 'Are you all right? You look a bit worried.'

'I'm not worried,' I said. 'I'm just tired.'

I mean, I'm NOT worried. Like I said, what would be the point?

And the last person in the world I'm going to be scared of is Mickey Martin.

THURSDAY 28TH MAY
To do: Move back into my room
Mood: Miz

4.00pm
I'm not in my cupboard any more. I'm in my room on my bunk. The top one. Jake slept in the underneath one.

He wanted to sleep in the top one but Auntie Janice thought he'd find some way of falling out in the night.

'He manages to fall out of most things,' she said.

I showed Jake the new car she'd given me before they went home.

I said, 'Do you want to see it go?'

He said, 'Yeeeahh!'

I drove it round and round the kitchen floor. Then we set up an obstacle course with my Lego and I tried to drive it in and out of the gaps. I wasn't very good. I kept crashing.

Every time I did, Jake shouted, 'Again! Again! Do crashing again!'

It made me think, though – if I decide not to be a sports journalist or a teacher, maybe I could be a rally driver. Now that would be cool.

4.30pm

I wish they hadn't gone. Mum said they could stay for the rest of the week if they wanted but Auntie Janice said she needed to get back.

When Jake got in the car he said, 'I don't want to be an elephant any more. I want to be Benny.'

That kid has got SO much sense.

5.00pm

This house is too quiet.

Where is Thomas the Tank Engine when you need him?

44

FRIDAY 29TH MAY

To do: Ring Danny and Paul
Mood: Too hot to have a mood

3.00pm

Scorching day. Been round at Paul's all morning.
Mum said she'd drop me off on her way to buy
new slippers. Danny came too. We were going
to play football but it was too hot.

Danny kept asking me if I was OK.

I said, 'Of course I'm OK. Why wouldn't I be?'

He said, 'You know, what with Mickey coming
back.'

I said, 'I really don't care about him. Can we
just not talk about it?'

Danny said, 'If that's what you want.'

I said, 'It is what I want. I'm fine. Stop asking.'

Then Paul said he'd been reading this book
about spies and wouldn't it be mega if all of us in
the Topz Gang had code names and we invented
our own language to communicate in. He said
he'd been thinking about it and he'd come up
with the code name Blueberry (well, this is Paul
we're talking about). Danny decided he'd like to
be Rat (because he's got a pet one) and I said I'd be Red
Zed (Red obviously because of the hair and Zed because
I didn't want to be just Red).

That was the easy bit. Then we had to come up
with a stonking good (and preferably uncrackable)

code. Six chocolate milkshakes, a box of choc ices and a lot of sucking on ice cubes later, we finally decided to write words down using numbers for each letter of the alphabet (instead of the letters obviously). But numbering A B C D as 1 2 3 4, etc was a bit simple, so Blueberry thought it would be fiendishly clever if we only used odd numbers and missed out number 1 altogether, as follows:

3	5	7	9	11	13	15	17	19	21	23	25	27
a	b	c	d	e	f	g	h	i	j	k	l	m

29	31	33	35	37	39	41	43	45	47	49	51	53
n	o	p	q	r	s	t	u	v	w	x	y	z

Rat said that if we put slashes after each full word then we'd know that was the end of that particular word.
  We tried it out:

Blueberry: 41 17 11 / 19 7 11 / 7 43 5 11 39 / 3 37 11 / 27 11 25 41 19 29 15.
  Rat: 19 / 23 29 31 47. / 19 / 41 17 19 29 23 / 19'27 / 39 19 41 41 19 29 15 / 31 29 / 31 29 11.
  Red Zed: 19 / 47 19 39 17 / 19 / 17 3 9 29'41 / 17 3 9 / 41 17 3 41 / 25 3 39 41 / 7 17 31 7 / 19 7 11. / 19 / 13 11 11 25 / 39 19 7 23.

Which translated means:

Blueberry: The ice cubes are melting.
Rat: I know. I think I'm sitting on one.
Red Zed: I wish I hadn't had that last choc ice. I feel sick.

It worked really brilliantly, it just took a very long time. Blueberry said we'd probably get quicker because, if we used it a lot, we'd start to remember which numbers stood for which letters.

We did try 'talking' in code by holding up the right number of fingers for each letter, but decided to scrap it. Not only did it get really complicated because you lost count all the time so you had to keep starting again, but also it was probably going to take about four hours every time you wanted to say something simple like, 'My bike's got a puncture.'

Blueberry said we could pass the code on to all the other Topz at youth club tonight. Then they could think up code names over the weekend and on Sunday at church it would be 3 25 25 / 39 51 39 41 11 27 39 / 15 31 (all systems go).

I said I wasn't sure if I'd be able to get there tonight. It's the bowling night that was put off from last week.

Rat said, 'We can always give you a lift.'

I said, 'No, it's not that, I've just got stuff to do ... probably. I mean, what with Jake and Auntie Janice going, my room's a right state.'

Blueberry said, 'Your room's always a right state.'

I said, 'Yeah, but at least it's _my_ right state. Mum's tidied up and now I can't find a thing.'

4.30pm

Mum's wearing her new slippers. They're pink and they've got ears. She's walking around with fluffy pink bunnies on her feet …

I think I need to go and lie down now.

7.30pm

Glad I didn't go out. Bowling's all right, I suppose, but I'm not really in the mood. I just fancied staying in.

The Dixons Gang often hang around at the bowling alley. Mickey Martin used to spend all his time with them but he's probably not bothered now he's back from Oz. I don't expect he'll be anywhere near there tonight. Even if he is, why should <u>I</u> be bothered? If he wants to creep about with a bunch of losers, it's got nothing to do with me.

I just didn't feel like bowling, that's all. I don't <u>always</u> have to go to youth club.

SUNDAY 31ST MAY

To do: Get ready for school tomorrow
Mood: Last day of half term-ish

2.30pm

After Sunday Club, Greg came over and asked if I was all right.

I said, 'Why is everyone so interested in how I am all of a sudden?'

He said, 'I'm always interested in you. We missed you at bowling on Friday, you know.'

I said, 'Yeah, sorry. I couldn't make it.'

He said, 'Look, Paul and Danny came to see me. They're worried about you.'

'Why?' I said. (I felt a bit annoyed. They're not going to let this Mickey Martin thing drop, are they?)

'They care about you,' Greg said. 'We all do.'

I just wanted to go home at that point.

I said, 'Nobody needs to be worried about me. If I've got a problem, it's up to me to sort it out, not anyone else. Anyway, as far as I know I haven't got any problems.'

'That's good,' Greg said, 'but if you find you have, just remember there are plenty of people around who can help. You're not on your own.'

'I know,' I said.

The trouble is when you're being bullied, that's exactly how you do feel – on your own. Totally.

I'm not letting it happen this time, though. I'm not even going to let it start. And anyway, like I keep telling everyone, for all we know Mickey Martin may not even be going to Holly Hill School.

4.30pm

Dad said, 'Is this a private bad mood or can anyone join in?'

I said, 'I'm not in a bad mood.'

He said, 'What would you call it then?'

I said, 'Thoughtful.'

He said, 'Well, there's nothing wrong with a bit of thoughtfulness. I get a bit thoughtful myself from time to time.'

I wish you'd get a bit thoughtful now, I thought, then maybe you'd stop talking and leave me alone.

He said, 'You know the best thing about thoughts?'

'No,' I said, but I had a horrible feeling I knew what he was going to say.

He said, 'They're so much better when you share them.'

Yup. I was right.

'I tell you what,' he said, 'if you tell me yours, I'll tell you mine.'

Aaaaaaaaaah! Why does he have to do this to me? How can you say, 'Look, I don't feel like talking to you so why don't you just leave me alone?' to a dad whose being Mr Kind and Understanding? I mean, is it right? Is it fair?

Then he said, 'You know you can always share your thoughts with God, don't you?'

I nodded. (If I said anything now he'd think I was cracking and then he'd never go away.)

'All right, then,' he said. 'I'm going downstairs. If you fancy a bit of chocolate fudge cake, there's some in the kitchen.'

That's the other thing grown-ups do when they're not getting their own way – try and win you over with chocolate fudge cake. Don't they realise that some things are bigger than food?

6.00pm

OK, OK, I admit it, I'm weak and pathetic. The cake thing worked. I only had three slices though, and the last one was quite thin and floppy.

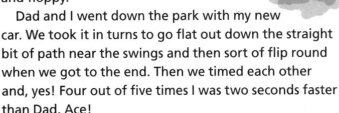

Dad and I went down the park with my new car. We took it in turns to go flat out down the straight bit of path near the swings and then sort of flip round when we got to the end. Then we timed each other and, yes! Four out of five times I was two seconds faster than Dad. Ace!

When we got back, Paul rang.

He said, 'Have you got a pen?'

I said, 'No, why?'

He said, 'Well get one so you can write down all the other Topz code names.'

I said, 'All right, ready.'

He said, 'Dave – 5 3 29 9 19 41.'

I said, 'What's that?'

He said, 'It's Dave's code name in code.'

I said, 'I know that, but what is his code name?'

He said, 'I don't want to say it over the phone. Someone might be listening.'

Sometimes I do worry about Paul.

The rest of the code names are:

John: 37 11 3 9 51 / 39 3 25 41 11 9 (Ready Salted)
Sarah: 7 3 41 (Cat)
Josie: 39 29 31 47 13 25 3 23 11 (Snowflake)
And Dave's is Bandit.

When I've memorised all the names, Paul says I have to destroy the piece of paper they're written on.

I said, 'Can't I just put it in the bin?'

He said, 'No. You'll have to eat it, or something.'

I said, 'Paul, don't you think you're taking this a bit too seriously?'

He said, 'No. If we're going to have a proper Topz code then it's got to be Topz secret!'

Completely bonkers if you ask me. (I didn't eat it. I tore it into tiny pieces, mixed them all up and put them in different bins round the house.)

8.30pm

Voting day for school mag editor tomorrow. At least I'm looking forward to that bit. Even if I decide not to be a sports journalist, I'm still going to be a fanstonkingtastic editor. I'm going to make that mag the best it's ever been. The first thing I'm going to do is change the name. At the moment it's called 'Holly Hill School Magazine' (yawn yawn). When I take over, it's going to be HOLLY HILL'S HOT SPOT. Teachers won't be asking, 'Have you got your school magazine?' any more, they'll be saying, 'Remember your copy of "Hot Spot"!' Cool, or what??

9.00pm

Mum said was I all ready for tomorrow. I said yes.

I'm not, though. I mean, I've got everything I need in my bag, but I just don't want to go.

Supposing Mickey IS there? Supposing nothing's changed and as soon as he sees me it all kicks off again? I think I'd rather spend the rest of my life with Mr Mallory rabbiting on about my hair than have Mickey breathing down my neck all over again. Why did they have to come back here? Aren't there enough other places in the world they could have gone?

Maybe I should have said something to Dad. I just don't want him and Mum to make a big thing out of something there may be no need to make a big thing about.

I think maybe I should tell them.

I think maybe I will.

10.30pm
Mum and Dad are so cool!

I told them about Mickey and Dad said, 'I thought that's what the problem was.'

I said, 'How did you know he was back?'

He said, 'I just had a feeling. Of course it helped when I bumped into Mickey's dad at the garage yesterday.'

Then Mum said everything I'd been thinking – just because they've moved back here, it doesn't mean Mickey'll be going to Holly Hill, and even if he does, he might well keep out of my way this time.

She said, 'Let's not make a problem out of it until we know there is one. It could all be fine.'

I said, 'I know. That's what I keep thinking. But then I start remembering how bad he made me feel last time and … I get worried.'

Mum said, 'I think this calls for that last bit of chocolate fudge cake.'

While she was in the kitchen, Dad said, 'I know things can be scary when you don't know how they're going to turn out. But it all got sorted last time and that's exactly what will happen this time. You've got a great, big God looking after you. You may think tomorrow's going to be full of nasty surprises but God's been there before you. He knows all about being bullied. Look what Jesus went through. He'd done nothing wrong but He was still picked on just because people didn't like some of the things He said. God's going to walk in with you through that school gate and He's going to stick like glue all day long.'

I said, 'Will He help me know what to do like He did last time?'

Dad said, 'He'll help you know exactly what to do. If anything happens, even if you just see Mickey across the cloakroom or something, just say quietly, 'Lord, thank You for being here with me. I need You to help me deal with this.' Then try and let Mickey see that you're not scared of him any more.'

'I am scared of him, though, Dad.'

'I know. So does God. That's why He's on your side.'

Thank You, Lord, for being on my side. (Just felt I needed to say that.)

MONDAY 1ST JUNE
Homework: None
To do: Nothing in particular
Mood: So so (whatever that means)

5.00pm
Mickey is coming back to Holly Hill. He's probably starting tomorrow. Mr Mallory told us this morning after registration. Apparently he's not going to be in my class, though. He's been put in the other year group. At least that's a plus. Dad was right. God has been there before me and He's sorted that bit out already. Mega.

The REALLY annoying thing about today was the mag voting. We were told we had all day to finish making up our minds and get our votes in. Then the votes would be counted tomorrow and the new editor announced in assembly on Wednesday afternoon. WEDNESDAY AFTERNOON!! That is yonks away! Teachers just have no idea what's important in life.

If I was sorting this out, I'd have all the votes in by lunchtime; I wouldn't bother with lunch, I'd spend my eating time counting them all; then I'd have a special assembly first thing this afternoon to tell everyone the results. Why is that so complicated? They could so easily have it all done in a day. I feel like saying, 'Just give me the votes and I'll count them if you can't be bothered.'

Mum says I've got to learn to be patient. No one, but NO ONE, understands how big this is for me.

5.30pm
Mum said, 'This'll cheer you up. I forgot to show you.'

She'd had a thank you letter from Auntie Janice about coming to stay, and with it in the envelope was a card from Jake that he'd made specially for me. On the front he's drawn a picture of Thomas the Tank Engine, only, instead of a nose, Jake's given him an elephant's trunk. Underneath, Auntie Janice has written 'Thomas the Tank Elephant', and inside she's put 'Benny is the best!'. Then Jake's managed to write his name with a big X for a kiss beside it.

That little kid is SUCH a cool dude.

6.30pm

Made a card for Jakey. I've drawn a picture of him and me with elephants' trunks instead of noses and we're both banging on Mum's saucepans with wooden spoons.

elephant trunk

At least, that's what it's meant to be. But I've been looking at it for the last twenty minutes and I don't think I've got it quite right. For a start, my legs are shorter than my arms and my head looks as if it's been stuck on the end of a long, thin pole instead of on a neck. And as for the wooden spoons, they're enormous compared with Jake and me. They look like road signs. I wouldn't like Jake to think it was OK to go around banging his mum's saucepans with road signs. So I've decided to label everything just to be safe. I've drawn arrows to all the relevant bits and I've written 'me', 'you', 'elephant trunks', 'upside down saucepans', and (to make it mega clear) 'these are wooden spoons not road signs'. I think that ought to do it.

7.00pm

All things considered, I've decided I'm definitely not doing any artwork for the HHHS ('Holly Hill Hot Spot'). Dad always says it's a good idea to think big, but at the same time you need to know your limitations. My drawing skills are nothing if not limited.

8.30pm

Dad said, 'Are you all right about tomorrow?'

I said, 'Yeah. God's stuck Mickey in a different class so I won't have to see him that much.'

Dad said, 'I know. Just checking.'

I said, 'I wonder what makes someone pick on someone else.'

He said, 'There could be lots of reasons. Maybe they've got problems at home so they take it out on someone who's not going to stand up to them. Maybe it makes them feel big. They think that bullying someone gives them some sort of power.'

I said, 'I wouldn't want power like that.'

Dad said, 'God wouldn't want you to have power like that either. The kind of power God wants us to have is the power to love each other and care about each other. He wants us to use His power to make each other feel good not bad.'

I said, 'I know! That's what I want to do with the magazine. I want everyone to read it and feel good.'

Dad said, 'Well, that's a great idea, but I think you should wait until all the votes have been counted before you start making too many plans.'

I said, 'Dad, I could be the best thing that's ever happened to that mag.'

He said, 'I'm sure you could. I just don't want you to be disappointed.'

Disappointed? How could I be disappointed? It's got to be me. No one in their right mind is going to be interested in a problem page.

POWER

TUESDAY 2ND JUNE
Homework: Read Chapter 4 of 'Treasure Island'
To do: Try and stop thinking about vote counting which is driving me bonkeroonies!
Mood: Surprisingly good (considering)

4.30pm
Saw Mickey in the cloakroom at break. He was eating a packet of crisps and messing about with some of his mates from before. I was going to try and sneak in and out without him seeing me but I got spotted.

Mickey stopped talking. We looked at each other.

He said, 'Benny.'

I said, 'Mickey.'

And that was it really.

He didn't sound Australian or anything. Maybe you have to live out there for longer.

6.00pm
Asked Mr Mallory after lunch if he knew whether the votes had been counted yet. He said he didn't, and even if he did, he couldn't give anything away until the new editor was announced tomorrow.

He said, 'It's good to see you're so keen, though. There's obviously a lot more going on under that hair than meets the eye.'

Thanks, Mr Mallory. (I think.)

8.00pm
Dad's gone to band practice. He's going to start playing bass guitar in church on Sunday mornings. He says he used to play years ago before he grew up and had to start being sensible.

When I told John he said, 'Wicked! I don't think MY dad would even know what to do with a guitar. He says he's tone deaf.'

I said, 'What does that mean?'

He said, 'I don't really know. But I think it must be something to do with the way that, when he sings in the shower, the cat hides behind the sofa. Sad, really.'

My dad doesn't sing in the shower.

I have so much to be grateful for.

WEDNESDAY 3RD JUNE

Homework: Don't know yet
To do: Stay calm (Mum says deep breathing helps)
Mood: MEGA jitters

7.45am

Today's the day. Next time I write in this diary it should be as the editor of 'Hot Spot'. If not, it'll be a crime. (Might give up on the deep breathing thing. Tried it out but got dizzy and fell over.)

5.00pm

It's official. Everyone in my school is totally, completely and STINKILY STARK RAVING BONKERS!

The crime of the century has now been committed: the votes have been counted and the new editor is Alison Filby. ALISON FILBY!!

Not that she isn't really nice and everything and she's got some mega cool roller blades, but come on, dudes! I mean, how could they? After everything I could have done for them. We had the chance to get a really

WOWZY mag going and what have they done? They've voted for problem pages, lots of truly painful girly stuff and a chance to write in with funny pet stories!

Not only that, but Alison wants to call it 'Holly Hill's Own'. I mean 'Holly Hill's Own' what? 'Holly Hill's Own Pile Of Rubbish', if you ask me. Not that anyone's interested in <u>my</u> opinion, obviously. Otherwise they wouldn't have voted in Alison Filby.

One thing's for sure. This is a fantastic day for Mr Mallory and Mickey Martin. I bet they loved it when the losers' names were read out. Score fifty trillion zillion points to them.

7.00pm

Dad said, 'It's not the end of the world.'

I said, 'How can you say that? I might have been the greatest sports journalist in the history of the universe, only now it's never going to happen.'

He said, 'Why's it never going to happen?'

I said, 'Because I'm not going to write one more single word for the rest of my life.'

Mum said, 'That could be tricky. What about school? Anyway, I thought you wanted to be a teacher.'

Have you noticed how something MASSIVE can happen and grown-ups just totally miss the point?

This is it. The end. I am never writing another word. Goodbye.

(Phone's going. If it's Alison Filby ringing to say sorry for stealing my life's dreams, I've left the planet.)

WOAH!

7.45pm

It wasn't Alison Filby, it was Greg. He said he'd been thinking about me since our little chat on Sunday and was just phoning to see how it was all going.

I told him my life had fallen down a hole.

He said, 'Oh dear. Do you want to talk about it?'

I said it was too late for words, but I told him anyway.

Then he said it was funny I should mention wanting to be editor of a magazine, because he'd been thinking recently that it would be a great idea to have a Sunday Club magazine, and he'd been wondering who he could ask to take it on.

I said, 'I might be interested. What kind of thing are you thinking of?'

He said, 'Oh, you know, something to keep everyone up to date with what's going on – what we're looking at in Sunday Club, a 'what's on soon' page, that sort of thing. It could have youth club stuff in too – maybe write-ups about things like the table tennis tournament. Do you fancy getting some ideas together?'

IS HE KIDDING??

I said, 'I'll get started right now. I've got a megatastic name for it already. You're going to love it.'

Greg said, 'What is it?'

I said, 'Are you ready? "Sunday Club Hot Spot".'

(I think he liked it.)

9.00pm

Dad said I've got to try not to get upset about things so easily. He said he knew the school magazine was important to me, but not being picked for editor wasn't worth giving up writing for. He thought Greg's idea was ace.

'You see,' he said. 'Sometimes things don't turn out the way we want them to, but that doesn't mean it's the end of life as we know it because suddenly God comes along with something else tucked up His sleeve. Something even better. You've just got to learn to trust Him more.'

I said, 'Don't you ever get really wound up about stuff?'

He said, 'Of course I do. I think everyone does. And that's when you have to say, "OK, Lord, whatever happens, I know you still want the best for my life. Please help me to trust you and to know that you've got everything under control."'

I said, 'I suppose I should have done that this morning. It's just that I wanted this so much, I didn't really think about whether it was what God wanted for me.'

Dad said, 'Never mind, you can relax now. You've got a better job.'

I said, 'Yeah. I tried that deep breathing thing Mum does, but I don't think I got it right.'

Dad said, 'I never get it right either. It makes me dizzy and I fall over.'

63

THURSDAY 4TH JUNE

Homework: Hopefully none – no time!
To do: Let all Topz know about 'Sunday Club Hot Spot'/ plan mag
Mood: Busy busy busy!

7.55am

Got up early so I could write a note about the new mag to give to all the Topz Gang at school. Thought it was a good time to try out our code:

7 3 25 25 19 29 15 / 3 25 25 / 41 31 33 53! / 15 37 11
15 / 47 3 29 41 39 / 27 11 / 41 31 / 39 41 3 37 41 / 43
33 / 3 / 39 43 29 9 3 51 / 7 25 43 5 / 27 3 15. / 3 19 51
31 29 11 / 47 3 29 41 / 41 31 / 17 11 25 33 / 31 43 41? /
37 11 9 / 53 11 9.

Which translated means: Calling all Topz! Greg wants me to start up a Sunday Club mag. Anyone want to help out? Red Zed.

(How did spies find the time to write in code? It's cool, but so SLOW!)

4.30pm

Alison Filby came up at break and said, 'Sorry about the mag and everything, but I just wanted you to know that I'll always look at anything you write for it and if there's a place for it, I'll put it in.'

If there's a place for it? Talk about smug! As if I'm going to bother to write anything for a magazine called 'Holly Hill's Own'.

I said, 'Thanks, Alison, but things have changed since yesterday and I'm going to be too busy to bother with your mag now.'

Sarah heard and said wasn't I being a bit unkind.

I said, 'No. It's the truth. I've got my own magazine to worry about. I'm not going to have any time for hers.'

'I know,' Sarah said, 'but you could have been a bit less snappy. It's not Alison's fault she got voted in instead of you.'

I said, 'It's got nothing to do with that. I've just got more important things to do now.'

Girls. They're so sensitive.

Anyway, all the Topz Gang want to be involved with MY new mag. We agreed we'd each write lots of ideas down after school, then discuss them at youth club tomorrow.

8.30pm

Saw Mickey at lunchtime. I was going into the library when he was coming out. He actually held the door open for me.

I said, 'Thanks.'

He said, 'No probs.'

I was so shocked I forgot why I'd gone to library in the first place.

SATURDAY 6TH JUNE

Homework: Make up crossword based on 'Treasure Island'
To do: Remind Greg about the 'what's on soon' list
Mood: Grunt

10.00am

Mag meeting at youth club went really badly. I don't know what's the matter with everybody. I went through all their ideas but, just because I decided not to use most of them, Josie said I was being bossy and if I didn't want anyone else's ideas, why had I bothered to ask for them in the first place?

I don't understand what she's on about. It's not as if I chucked them all out. Dave suggested having a contents page so I said we could do that, and Paul said the letter 'O' of the word 'Hot' on the cover ought to be big, red and glowy-looking to look like a hot spot (obviously because of the mag name), so I said we'd do that too. Just because I'd rather stick with my ideas for the rest of it, why does that make me bossy?

Josie said, 'Greg may have asked you to run this magazine, but that doesn't make it your personal property. If you're not interested in sharing it then I'm not interested in doing it.'

Sarah said, 'Neither am I,' and they stomped off.

They just don't like it because Greg asked me to be in charge and not them – which is SO pathetic.

Even John said maybe it would be better if I did it on my own.

Thanks a lot, guys.

12.15pm

Rang Greg to remind him about doing the 'what's on soon' list.

He said he'd heard we'd all had a bit of a fall out.

I said, 'What do you mean?'

He said, 'I had a chat with Josie.'

I said, 'It's not MY fault. They're the ones who are being unfair. I've asked them to help, but if they don't want to that's up to them.'

Greg said, 'It's not that they don't want to help. I think they just feel as though you're pushing them out.'

I said, 'That is SO not true. They're just jealous.'

'Look,' Greg said, 'this is a magazine for Sunday Club. That means anyone can contribute to it. It's not your magazine. What you've got is a really important job which is about organising things and pulling them all together. But it's also about finding a way to include other people who want to be involved.'

I said, 'But most of their ideas are rubbish.'

He said, 'Benny, no one's ideas are rubbish. You mustn't look down on people just because their thoughts are different to yours. God values all of us. Even though we're always getting things wrong, He doesn't sit there and criticise us for them. All the time He's looking for the good things in us, the positive things. And that's what He wants us to look for in each other.'

How come Greg's making it look as if this is MY fault?

12.30pm
This is **SO** not my fault.

It isn't.

I've been thinking about it and it definitely isn't.

Definitely.

12.45pm
Going to tell Greg tomorrow he can keep his magazine. I'm going to be a teacher. (Or a rally driver.)

8.00pm
Asked Mum if I could miss church tomorrow and, of course, she wanted to know why. I told her they were all ganging up on me and she wouldn't believe me. I said it was true – they all think I'm bossy and horrible because Greg's put me in charge of the magazine. Even Greg thinks I'm bossy and horrible.

She said, 'I'm sure he doesn't. Anyway we can't not

go. It's Dad's first Sunday playing with the band.'

I said, 'How can he be playing with the band already? He's only been to one practice.'

She said, 'I know. Clever, isn't he?'

Great. Not only do I have to face Greg and everyone in the morning knowing they hate me, I also have to suffer the embarrassment of my dad on the platform up the front totally mucking it up on the bass guitar.

I said, 'All right, I'll go, but only if I can sit at the back in a sack.'

She said, 'Whatever makes you feel comfortable, Benjamin.'

Oh ha ha ha.

8.45pm

Greg rang. Mum answered. As soon as I knew it was Greg I started mouthing (incredibly clearly so she couldn't possibly have misunderstood), 'I'm not talking to him. Say I've gone to bed.'

Mum said, 'Hold on a minute, Greg, Benny's trying to say something.'

Is it me or do grown-ups have a part of their brain missing?

I was about to say I wasn't going to have anything to do with the mag any more and I was only coming to church tomorrow because Dad thinks he can play the guitar, when Greg said (out of the blue and quite selfishly really because it meant I couldn't say what I was going to say) that he was sorry about what had happened with the other Topz and he felt it was his fault.

What?

He said he should have thought things through more before mentioning the magazine idea to me, and what he ought to have done was write down a list of jobs and see who there was at Sunday Club who'd be interested in doing them.

I knew it, I thought. He doesn't want me to run it any more anyway.

'So what I'd like to do now, if it's all right with you,' he said, 'is to have you as the magazine's chief editor so that basically you're running it, you write a regular newsy kind of letter to go at the beginning of each issue, and you're responsible for getting all the bits and pieces together. Then I'm going do a list of other jobs and see what names go up.'

'What other jobs?' I said. (I wasn't agreeing to anything. Yet.)

'Things like events writer, what's on officer, publicity officer so people know the magazine's coming out, games page writer, youth club co-ordinator. You can put your name up for other jobs too, if you like. I want this to be a magazine for Sunday Club by Sunday Club. But it needs you to bring it all together.'

I still wasn't agreeing to anything.

He said, ' So. Are you up for it?'

I said, 'Yeah, maybe. I might. Probably.'

Sometimes it's hard to be decisive.

'Is that a yes then?' Greg said.

'I ...'

'Good. See you in the morning, Benny.'

Pushy, or what?

9.00pm

Dad's in the kitchen polishing his guitar.
Now I'm REALLY worried.

9.30pm

Told God I was sorry for criticising my friends. I hadn't
really realised that's what I was doing till Greg said.

I said, 'Lord God, I know You value all of us. I know
You even value me when I'm horrible. I'm sorry for
saying my friends' ideas were rubbish. They weren't
rubbish at all. The only rubbish around is inside me for
wanting to feel important because I was the one Greg
asked to run the magazine. Help me to value people like
You do and to look for what's good in them instead of
criticising them.'

(Still not sure about Dad's bass guitar playing though.)

SUNDAY 7TH JUNE

Homework: As Saturday
To do: Homework
Mood: Surprised (in a surprisingly good way)

8.30pm

Ten surprising things that have happened today:

1. Woke up in a good mood.
2. Dad's guitar playing wasn't a total embarrassment.
3. Josie and Sarah said they were sorry for stomping off on Friday.
4. I said to Josie and Sarah I was sorry for being bossy.
5. I actually admitted to being bossy.
6. None of the Topz Gang hate me – they think I'll make a great editor.
7. Magazine officially named 'Sunday Club Hot Spot'.
8. Danny's invited me to go quad biking on his birthday (next Sunday).
9. Spoke to Jake on the phone and he said I was his favourite elephant.
10. Decided to say sorry to Alison Filby tomorrow for being off with her because of the mag voting.

8.45pm

Paul rang. He said he'd put his name up on Greg's jobs list to interview people and please could he make a time to interview Dad about being a rock guitarist.

8.55pm

Paul rang. He said, if he couldn't interview Dad, please could he interview me instead about being a magazine editor.

9.00pm

Paul rang. He said, if I didn't want to be interviewed, please could he interview Mum about what it's like to live with a rock guitarist and a magazine editor.

I said (kindly), 'Paul, I don't think anyone's going to be that interested.'

He said, 'OK.'

WEDNESDAY 10TH JUNE

Homework: None
To do: Decide what to get Danny for his birthday
Mood: Normal

8.30pm

Went round to Dave's after school.

Played Cluedo, then Dave said, 'When you grow up, if you could have any car in the world, what would it be?'

I said, 'I don't know. I think I'd like a Land Rover.'

He said, 'I'd like to build my own.'

I said, 'Really?'

He said, 'Yeah.'

I said, 'Do you know how?'

He said, 'No, but it can't be that difficult and my uncle's got his own garage.'

I said, 'You know Ryan in your class? His dad's got a garage.'

He said, 'I didn't know that.'

I said, 'He was crying in the toilets at lunchtime.'

Dave said, 'Who? Ryan's dad?'

'No. Not his dad. Ryan.'

'Why?'

'I don't know,' I said. 'He wouldn't tell me.'

'He seemed all right this afternoon.'

I said, 'I found him crying in the toilets on Monday too.'

'Weird,' said Dave.

'That's what I thought,' I said.

9.00pm

Weekend's looking mega. School disco on Friday then quad biking on Sunday.

I said to Mum, 'I don't know what to get Danny for his birthday.'

She said, 'What ideas have you got?'

I said, 'The only thing I can think of is a quad bike.'

She said, 'You'd better keep thinking then.'

THURSDAY 11TH JUNE

Homework: Spellings
To do: Persuade Mum to ring Danny's mum (or dad)
Mood: Still normal (well, normal for me)

7.00pm
Finally got Mum to ring Danny's mum.

She said, 'Why can't you do it?'

I said, 'Because if I ring up and Danny answers and I ask to speak to his mum, he's going to think it's a bit weird. But if <u>you</u> ring up and ask to speak to his mum, he'll think you're just ringing for a chat or something.'

Mum said, 'Mmm, or something.'

I said, 'Then you can ask what we could get him for his birthday without him suspecting anything.'

When she came off the phone she said, 'An electric guitar strap.'

I said, 'Why would he want an electric guitar strap?'

Mum said, 'To put on his electric guitar.'

I said, 'Danny hasn't got an electric guitar.'

Mum said, 'No, but he will have. That's what his mum and dad are giving him for his birthday.'

I said, 'Are you sure? I never knew Danny wanted to play the guitar.'

She said she was absolutely positive, although she did have to ask Danny's mum to repeat it three times because Danny was in the next room and she was trying to speak quietly so he wouldn't hear.

So, Danny's a secret rocker. Which is almost as shocking as Dad being a secret rocker. (Actually, no, it's not.)

Dad says we can go and buy a strap on Saturday morning so I can give it to Danny when we go quad biking on Sunday. He said it would give him the opportunity to check out bass guitars.

I said, 'Dad, you're not going to play any in the shop, are you?'

He said, 'I'll have a twiddle about if I see something I like.'

Terrific. I am SO going to regret this.

SATURDAY 13TH JUNE

Homework: Draw treasure map/spellings
To do: Too much
Mood: Zippety-doo-dah!

10.00am

So much to say. So little time to say it.
School disco details later. Got to go and hang around in music shops with Dad now. Sigh.

3.00pm

That is it. I am never going shopping with my dad ever again for as long as I live. Not even if he pays me. I'd rather have no money and live on lentils.

We were in the music shop and I picked up a guitar strap and said, 'This one looks OK. Can we go now?'

But it was never going to be that easy. Dad had that 'come on, Benny, don't rush me' look. He was having a good old peer at the bass guitars when the shop assistant came over.

No, I thought, please no.
Too late.

The shop assistant said, 'We've got a good range in at the moment. Are you looking for anything in particular?'

'Not really,' Dad said. 'I just thought I'd see what's out there. Mine's pretty old, that's all. It's been tucked away in a cupboard for years.'

Best place for it, I thought.

Are shop assistants blind? Don't they notice when their customers' children are silently but frantically trying to warn them to keep well away, and under no circumstances to utter the dreaded words, 'Feel free to try out anything you like'? Do they honestly think we've got nothing better to do than stand around and listen while our dads pretend they know everything there is to know about bass guitars, and then try to cover up the fact that actually they know nothing at all by saying, 'Whoops. As I said, I am a bit rusty'?

Mum said, 'You've been gone a long time.'

I said, 'Yes. It's amazing how long it takes to try out every guitar in a music shop and then have a "quick fiddle" on the drum kit in the window on the way out.'

Mum said, 'Oh, good. You had fun then.'

I said, 'No. Dad had fun. I just had earache.'

3.30pm

Done Danny a birthday card. I put: To Rat. Hope you like your present. You have no idea what I went through to get it. Red Zed.

(I was going to do it in code but I couldn't be bothered.)

5.00pm

School disco was fab, wild, ace, triff! I was a bit worried about going because of Mickey. Not that he'd probably start anything, I just don't like being where he is. But Paul said earlier he'd heard him saying in the cloakroom that he wasn't going to waste his time going to some stupid, little kids disco. So I sort of thought he wouldn't be there, and he wasn't.

Unfortunately Mr Mallory was.

He said, 'Benny! So glad to see you brought your hair with you.'

Does that man never know when to stop?

The DJ was mega! He got up and showed us some wicked dance moves. Then he ran a contest. We had to do the dance in groups of five or six and he said the winning group would be the one with the best groove. Our group was me, Danny, John, Paul, Sarah and (believe it or not) Alison Filby! We didn't win but I think we should have done. Sarah and Alison were really good, but on one of the twisty round bits, my shoelace got caught under Danny's foot and I fell over. We managed to carry on dancing, though. Josie said it wasn't THAT noticeable, I just looked a bit surprised.

But talk about sweaty! Sarah said I had a face like a beetroot and Paul was so hot his glasses kept steaming up. I said he needed little windscreen wipers, and we

all fell about laughing. Paul said I needed a shower because I smell.

Fair enough.

Guess what, though? Just before she went home, Alison came up to me and said I seemed to be having such a good time, how would I feel about doing a write-up of the disco for 'Holly Hill's Own'. I didn't want her to think I was still being offy about not being the editor, and she is a really good dancer. So I said I was quite busy because I was working on another magazine now, but I'd give it a go – at least I tried to say that, but I could hardly breathe because I'd just been doing pretend stunt fighting with Paul for the last ten minutes, and I probably sounded a bit funny.

Still, she said, 'Thank you,' and gave me a huge smile, so I'm guessing she could understand my huffing and puffing (and wheezing and choking).

Dad picked me up and we gave Paul a lift home.

I said, 'Bye, Paul. See you Sunday.'

He said, 'Bye, Benny.'

Then he said to Dad, 'Oh, by the way, if Benny seems really happy, it's because he's got a girlfriend.'

I said, 'Paul, Alison Filby is NOT my girlfriend.'

Paul just grinned and said, 'Yeah, right.'

Dad had his eyebrows raised. I was in the back of the car but I could see that they were in the 'up' position in the mirror. He didn't say anything.

Probably just as well.

6.00pm

I can't help thinking about Ryan in Dave's class. He wasn't at the disco. Dave said he asked him if he was going but Ryan said he couldn't make it.

I only saw him once yesterday, at lunchtime. He was on his own round the back of the changing huts.

I've just got this niggly feeling about him. There's something going on, I know there is.

8.00pm

Greg rang. He said he'd been through the lists he put up last week and sorted out who's doing what for 'Hot Spot'.

Manager: Him
Editor: Me
Publicity: Josie, Sarah, Pete and Megan
Feature writers/ interviews: Danny, Paul and Charlotte
What's on: Dave and Eddie
Games/jokes page writers: John, Paul and me
Youth Club correspondents: Susie, Sarah, Josie and Rhianna

I said, 'What does the manager do?'

Greg said, 'Not a lot. Just keeps an eye on how it's all going. Are you happy with that?'

I said, 'Yup, fine,' so he's going to get the list typed up and give everyone a copy tomorrow. He said the next thing to do would be to arrange a meeting to decide when the first issue was coming out and what was going in it.

Wow. I've got to write up the school disco, do my homework, wrap up Danny's guitar strap, go to church, go quad biking and plan out the first issue of 'Hot Spot'.
Pressure pressure!

SUNDAY 14TH JUNE

Homework: Done treasure map/still got spellings
To do: Everything
Mood: Definitely stressy

9.30am

Dad says I look stressed. I told him I'd got so much stuff to do I didn't know where to start. He said I had to learn to prioritise.

I said, 'What's that in English, please, Dad?'

He said, 'You need to make a list of all the things you've got to do, decide which are most important and concentrate on doing those first. Then you can tick them off as you get through them.'

Mum said (not very helpfully), 'I make lists all the time, but I make sure I always include lots of things I've already done so my lists have plenty of ticks on them to start with.'

When I've worked out what the point of that is, I'm sure I'll find it very useful. (Not.)

In fact, I don't think I'm a 'list' sort of person. It's probably one of those things where either you are or you aren't. I suppose it is sort of satisfying ticking off stuff like homework. Maybe that's how it starts. You think you're not a list person but slowly, bit by bit, without even realising it a lot of the time, you start making lists of this and lists of that, until one day you wake up and the first thing you do is reach for a pen and say to yourself, 'Oh, goody, let's make a list of everything I've got to do today.'

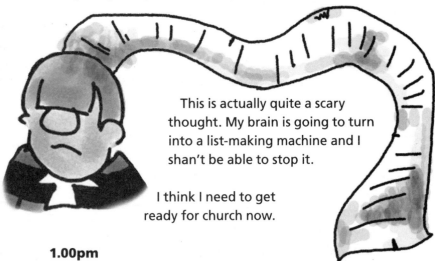

This is actually quite a scary thought. My brain is going to turn into a list-making machine and I shan't be able to stop it.

I think I need to get ready for church now.

1.00pm
We're going to have our first 'Hot Spot' meeting an hour before youth club next Friday. We've got to meet round at Greg's and bring our ideas with us, which is great because it gives me all week to plan something out and I'll be able to get through some of the other things on my list first. (Aaaah! List! You see? It's happening already.)

Paul said he'd got another great idea for an interview.

I said, 'What?'

He said, 'I could interview you about what it's like to have a girlfriend.'

I said, 'I could interview you about what it's like to have no brain.'

7.30pm

STONKER of a day!

Quad biking is just <u>MEGA SUPER COOL!</u>

I'm going to keep on being editor of 'Hot Spot' and all that because it wouldn't be fair to let everyone down now, but actually I've definitely decided I'm going to be a rally driver. I've only been quadding once before and it was ages ago. Danny goes quite often and I <u>still</u> managed to overtake him on the bends. Even the guy in charge said I could probably be a natural with a bit more practice.

Sarah and John could really shift round the track too. Paul managed to fall off but he said he did it on purpose – and knowing Paul he probably did.

We hadn't been there long when, guess what? Ryan arrived with his dad. It turns out he's a pretty ace driver.

(Ryan, that is, not his dad. His dad's OK but Ryan's well nippy. I couldn't beat him on the bends.)

When it was time to go, Danny asked him if he'd like to come back with us to his house for pizza. First of all he said he didn't think he could, but then his dad said why not go and have some fun and he'd pick him up later, so in the end he came.

Danny showed us his guitar and his mum helped him put the new strap on.

I said, 'How come you never said you were learning guitar?'

Danny said, 'I thought you might think I was a bit of a geek.'

I said, 'Danny, some of the most famous people in the world play guitar. I think it's really cool.'

Paul said, 'Do you think it's cool that your dad plays guitar?'

I said, 'Dad doesn't exactly "play" guitar. He just sort of thumps it a bit.'

Josie said, 'Well I think your dad's really great. Grown-ups should do stuff like that if they want to.'

I said, 'Really?'

Josie said, 'Yeah. Being grown-up isn't just about being old and boring. There are lots of things I'm going to do when I grow up. I've got a great long list.'

(There it is again, the 'list' word. Is there no escape?)

The pizza was amazing. Danny's mum makes it

herself. She's one of those healthy eating people. Danny always has carrot sticks in his lunch box.

I said to him once, 'Don't you worry that one night you'll go to bed as you but when you wake up, you'll find you've turned into a rabbit?'

Danny said, 'Don't you worry that every night you go to bed as you and when you wake up, you're still you?' (Uh?)

When Ryan's dad came to pick him up, Ryan said, thanks, he'd had a really good time. I said why didn't he hang out with us at lunchtimes if he wanted and he said, yeah, maybe he would.

Then he said something weird.

He said, 'You lot all go to church, don't you?'

Sarah said, 'Yes. Why, do you?'

Ryan said, 'No. It's just – you all seem to have a really good laugh. I didn't think you'd be like that.'

'What did you think we'd be like?' Sarah asked.

Ryan said, 'I don't know. A bit serious, I suppose.'

Paul said, 'Serious? Us? Ryan, it's people like us who invented laughter.' At which point we all fell about – including Ryan.

After he'd gone, Josie said, 'Do you think that's what everyone thinks? That Christians are just boring and fuddy-duddy?'

'I don't know,' I said. 'I never really thought about it.'

'Well, I think we should ALL think about it,' Sarah said. 'If people think we're boring, they're going to think Jesus is boring too, and He so isn't.'

Dave said, 'Maybe we should invite Ryan to Sunday Club. Or at least to youth club.'

'Yeah, I think we should,' I said. 'And if he won't come, we can always kidnap him. Just for a laugh.'

8.30pm

I thought I ought to tell Mum and Dad that I'd come to a decision about my future.

I said, 'Mum, Dad, when I grow up I'm going to be a rally driver.'

Dad said, 'What happened to being a sports journalist?'

Mum said, 'And there was me thinking you were going to be a teacher.'

I said, 'I've just got to do what's right for me.'

Mum said, 'Of course you have, Benny.'

I said, 'If I do change my mind again, which I'm not going to, there is something else I might be quite good at.'

Dad said, 'What's that?'

I said, 'Pizza chef.'

Dad said, 'Why stick with pizzas? Why not go all out and buy a chip shop?'

Sometimes I don't think my parents take me seriously.

TUESDAY 16TH JUNE
Homework: Write a description of a pirate ship (why?)
To do: Mag planning
Mood: Not sure

5.00pm

Gave Alison my disco write-up. She said thanks and then smiled at me showing huge amounts of teeth. Paul says girls only show huge amounts of teeth when they smile if they really like you.

I said, 'Why would Alison Filby like me?'

Paul said, 'I've been asking myself that same question.'

I would have hit him but he was carrying his plasticine octopus. (His class are building a 3D under-the-sea display with Mrs Parker. Mr Mallory never does anything interesting like that.)

6.30pm

I've still got that niggly feeling. About Ryan. I didn't spot him anywhere around at lunchtime today or yesterday. I even went to look behind the changing huts, but he wasn't there. The only time I saw him was in the cloakroom when I got in this morning. I said hi. He said hi back, but kept his head down and didn't hang about. I'm sure he'd been crying again.

I want to be wrong. I REALLY want to be wrong. But somehow I just don't think I am.

8.00pm

Paul rang. He said this time he really had got a fantastic interview lined up for the mag, plus he'd got a sensational title for the interview bit of each issue.

I said, 'Go on, then.'

He said, 'Are you ready?'

I said, 'Ready as I'll ever be.'

He said, 'OK. We can call the interview page "Who's on the Hot Spot?" Get it? "Hot Spot"? Name of the mag and all that?'

I said, 'Yes, Paul, I get it. That's not bad.' (Pretty good actually.)

He said, 'Not bad? Wait till you hear the next bit. The first interviewee to go on the Hot Spot for the first ever issue of Sunday Club's first ever magazine is going to be … JESUS!'

It was one of those moments when you know you ought to sound really pleased and excited but somehow when you open your mouth, you just don't.

I said, 'Jesus?'

He said, 'Yeah! Inspired or what?'

I said, 'Definitely. Fantastic.' (I was trying to be enthusiastic, but kind at the same time.) 'Don't you think there might just be one tiny problem with interviewing Jesus, though?'

'No,' Paul said. 'What?'

I said, 'Well, you can't actually "interview" Him, can you? I mean, I know we talk to Him and everything and He listens and gives us answers, but that's not really like sitting in the same room with someone and interviewing them. Is it?'

Paul said, 'Have you got a brain or is it just a radish? You've got to use your imagination in this game. Of course I'm not ACTUALLY going to interview Him. But I'm going to write an interview with Him, asking Him questions and stuff and using what I know about Him to give the answers.'

I still wasn't really sure, so I just said, 'Oh,' in an interested sort of way.

Paul said, 'So? What do you think?'

'I think …' I said, 'I think … it's really … unusual.'

Paul said, 'Cool. That's exactly what I want it to be. Unusual. Thanks. I'll go and get started.'

I put the phone down. He's a nutter. Even someone with a radish for a brain can see that. Still, on the bright side, with people like Paul around, how could anyone seriously think Christians are boring?

8.15pm

Been thinking about my first editor's letter. I think maybe I'm going to write about showing the world that Christians do have fun. Sarah's right. If we're supposed to be trying to be like Jesus and people think we're just boring, then that's what they're going to think of Jesus too. And why would they want to be friends with someone who's boring?

9.00pm

Dad said, 'You look worried. Not still feeling stressed, are you?'

I said, 'No, it's not that. I've just got something on my mind, that's all.'

He said, 'Can I help?'

I said, 'It's not really up to me to talk about it. Anyway, it could be nothing.'

Dad said, 'You obviously don't think it's nothing or it wouldn't be on your mind.'

I said, 'OK. What should you do if you think someone's being bullied?'

He said, 'Are you talking about you and Mickey Martin?'

I said, 'No, it's not me. If it was me I'd have told you. I learnt that last time. I think Mickey might have started on someone else.'

'Why?' Dad said. 'Have you seen something happen?'

I said, 'No. This boy's not even in my class. There's just something about the way he is. And I've noticed he's been crying a bit.'

Dad said, 'Lots of things make people cry, not just being bullied.'

'I know,' I said. 'That's why I don't know what to do. It's just that, if he is having trouble with Mickey, he's probably too scared to tell, like I was. I don't even think he's got that many friends. He hasn't been at Holly Hill long. I know he wasn't there before Mickey went to Australia.'

Dad said, 'Well, it wouldn't be right to jump to conclusions. And even if he is being bullied, it may be nothing to do with Mickey Martin.'

'I know,' I said. 'So what should I do?'

Dad said, 'You can pray for him. That's always the best place to start. And you can let him know you're his friend. Then, if he wants to talk to someone, maybe he'll feel he can talk to you. After all, with what you went through with Mickey, if anyone can help him, you can.'

For an older person who's trying to be a rocker, Dad can actually be incredibly sensible and understanding.

9.45pm

Can't sleep tonight. I feel horrible. Horrible inside. Sad, somehow. I can't stop thinking about the way Mickey used to make me feel. Worthless. I didn't know how to talk to anyone. I wanted to hide away.

Just like Ryan's doing.

He's being bullied, I'm sure of it.
But if he won't talk to me, how can I help him?

WEDNESDAY 17TH JUNE

Homework: Finish pirate ship thing/Maybe something else
To do: Pray for Ryan/Talk to Dave about him
Mood: Worried

8.00am

Prickly eyes this morning. I couldn't get to sleep for ages and when I did it can only have been for about five minutes, then my alarm woke me up.

I prayed a lot for Ryan while I was lying in bed, though. I asked God to look after him and to show me how to help him, plus I asked Him how I could let Ryan know I want to be his friend.

No one deserves to be made to feel bad about themselves. God hates it. It's scary but I can't just take no notice. I can't pretend nothing's going on. It wouldn't be fair to Ryan. Or to God.

In the Bible, Jesus says that whenever we do something good for someone else, we're doing it for Him. That's why

I've got to help Ryan. God sorted things out when they were bad for me and He'll sort them out for Ryan too. It's what He does. One way or another, if we trust Him, He always finds a way to work things out.

5.00pm
Asked Dave if he knew much about Ryan. He said no, not really, except that his parents are divorced and he lives with his dad.

Then he said, 'Why do you want to know?'

I said, 'No reason. I just thought it'd be cool to get to know him a bit. I've got to prove to him going to church doesn't make you boring.'

It's not that I don't want Dave to know that Ryan may be having trouble with Mickey. It just doesn't seem right to talk about it with anyone before I've been able to talk about it with Ryan. And that's the bit I know is going to be really tricky. If something IS going on and he feels anything like I did, I bet he won't want to say anything to anyone.

But, guess what? We started practising for sports day this afternoon – which gave me a mega brilliant idea for how I could try and show him I want to be his friend.

First of all, we had to try out some of the wacky team games we always do. Bleahh. I reckon the teachers spend all year thinking them up. Then they sit round a table and have a big meeting to decide on the five most embarrassing ones.

Dad always says, 'Oh, come on, it's great fun. Where's your sense of humour?'

It's so much easier to have a sense of humour about our school's team games when you're watching them rather than when you're being forced to take part, I've noticed.

Anyway, to start off with, we all got split into groups in our team colours (I'm in yellows), then we had to practise following loads of crazy instructions. For example:

1. Grab a hat from the pile and put it on. (Not as easy as it sounds – the hats turned out either to be so big they fell over your eyes all the time, or so small you hadn't got a hope of keeping them on your head. No doubt Mr Mallory found that extremely amusing.)
2. Run up to the chair and sit down.
3. Put on the pair of wellies by the chair. (Again, it could all have been so simple if the wellies actually fitted. They didn't. They were like buckets and must have been at least four sizes bigger than your actual feet even with plimsolls on. Another good laugh for Mr Mallory.)
4. Jump in and out of a row of hoops laid flat on the ground. (It's almost impossible to drag one foot behind the other when you're wearing buckets on your feet. So jumping? They have got to be kidding!)
5. Pick up a beanbag and throw it into the box. (At this point, you're actually so busy worrying how you're going to manage to finish the game at all if you have to wear those wellies for much longer that you're hardly likely to get the beanbag anywhere near the box.)

6. Run (oh ha ha) back to the chair and take off the wellies.
7. Tear back to the next person in your team, give them the hat, then join the back of the line. (And if you're <u>really</u> lucky and everyone manages to whip through all of that super fast, you get to do the whole thing again – whoop-de-doo!)

The winning group is apparently the one with the most beanbags in the box when the whistle blows.

I'm sorry, but games like this are just so totally crushing if you're a serious sportsman. How do they come up with this stuff anyway? (I blame Mr Mallory.)

Only after we've been made to look like complete nerdy idiots in front of all our parents (not to mention each other) do we get to do the REAL sporty stuff – the races.

I usually do the boys' sprint, the boys' long distance, the relay and the three-legged dash. I tried the hurdles one year but it was a disaster. Paul said I wasn't jumping high enough, but I said it's not that, it's my feet. They're always getting in the way because they've grown too quickly so they're too long.

Paul said, 'If they were any smaller you'd probably just fall over all the time.'

I said, 'Your feet are smaller than mine and you don't fall over all the time.'

Paul said, 'Yes, but scientifically speaking, my feet are probably the right size for my body.'

I asked, 'If we're speaking scientifically, can the same be said of your brain?'

I always do the three-legged race with Danny. We tend to do pretty well, and usually finish somewhere in the first three. (I think it's because our legs are about the same length so we manage to get a good rhythm going.) Anyway – and this is where my stonking good idea about Ryan comes in – I decided to see if it would be OK with Danny if I asked Ryan to do it with me this year instead. (Ryan's in yellows too.) I said it would be a fantastic opportunity to show him that I'm just as bonkers as all his other mates.

I think Danny was a bit disappointed, but he was really great about it anyway. He said I was right and I couldn't pass up the chance to show Ryan just how loony and un-boring Christians can be – and, of all the Christians he knew, I was probably the most loony and possibly the most un-boring too.

I said, 'Only possibly?'

He said, 'Yeah. Sometimes you do go on a bit.'

(Must remember not to go on a bit when I'm around Ryan.)

So I bounced up to Ryan and said, 'Ryan! How do you fancy teaming up with one of Holly Hill's top three-leggers for the three-legged race?'

He looked a bit doubtful and said, 'Who do you mean?'

I said, 'Who do you think? Me, of course.'

He said, 'Oh. I don't know.'

'Come on,' I said, 'it'll be a right laugh. If you're half as zippy three-legging it as you are quad biking, we are going to rock this place!'

He still didn't look too sure. Inside I was going, 'Please, Lord God, please let him say yes.'

Ryan said, 'Can I think about it?'

'Do you have to?' I said. 'Can't you just say yes now?'

He said, 'I'll probably be rubbish.'

I said, 'Not a chance. You'll be with me, won't you? You are going to be training with the master.'

I suppose that was a bit over the top. Maybe I was being too pushy. Worse – maybe I was starting to go on a bit! Ugh. Just say yes, please say yes.

'Um...' he said.

'Yes?'

'OK.'

YESSSSS! Thank You, Lord.

I said, 'Ryan, you are not going to regret this. You and me, we're going to be legends.' (Three-legends actually. Tee hee hee. Well, I thought it was funny.)

Talk about cool bananas! We did it. God and me. Phase 1 of Operation Rescue Ryan now complete. Of course, I'm still not definitely sure that he needs rescuing, but I'm ALMOST definitely sure. And I'm almost definitely sure who he needs rescuing from.

Anyway, if I'm totally wrong about everything, I can still invite him along to Sunday Club. When he realises that being a Christian isn't about being boring and fudge-faced, he might even decide he wants to be friends with Jesus too. Then Jesus will rescue him from his old life and give him a brand, spanking new one. So it's Operation Rescue Ryan whichever way you look at it.

8.00pm

Danny rang.

He said, 'How did it go with Ryan?'

I said, 'How could he refuse? This is ME we're talking about.'

Danny said, 'Exactly. That's what's been worrying me.'

'Thanks,' I said.

THURSDAY 18TH JUNE

Homework: Maths sheet
To do: Finish mag planning
Mood: Buzz buzz buzz!

8.00pm

Think I've finally cracked what could go in the first 'Hot Spot', as follows:

Front cover – title (obviously) plus photo Greg took of everyone in table tennis tournament

Editor's letter

What's On

Greg's Greetings (Greg's teachy bit on something from the Bible)

Who's On The Hot Spot? (Paul's big interview – still not sure about the interview with Jesus, but it's definitely original)

Games/jokes page (Wordsearch/Bible quiz/at least four jokes)

Book review (If Paul's doing the interview, maybe Danny or Charlotte could do a book)

Back cover – Youth Club News Round-up (Reports on table tennis and bowling)

I've got more ideas for my editor's letter. I'll do a bit of an introduction first, to let everyone know what 'Sunday Club Hot Spot' is all about. I might ask for ideas for the mag too. Maybe we could put out a suggestions box. I'll see Greg tomorrow.

Then I'm not just going to write about showing the world that being a Christian is fun. I'm going to write about how Christians need to be different in lots of ways. How they need to stand out from the crowd and try to make friends with people – all sorts of people – and help them when they're in trouble. God loves everybody and that's what He wants us to do too. And if we can try and love everybody and do good things for them, it's got to make a difference.

That's how people who think Christians are boring will see that, actually, living for Jesus is OK. In fact it's better than OK. And when they realise how cool it is, hopefully they'll want to be Christians too. Which is what I'm praying for Ryan. If he knows God's on his side he might not be so scared to talk about what's happening.

(I could go on and on, but I haven't finished my homework and my maths sheet's calling to me. Thanks, Mr Mallory.)

love everybody

9.10pm

ORR (Operation Rescue Ryan) update: Managed to get Ryan to do a bit of three-legged training with me at lunchtime round the corner from the climbing frame. He said he didn't want to do it on the field because some of the other boys were playing football and we'd just be in the way. I noticed Mickey was in goal. Not that I suppose that means a lot.

There was only one problem. We didn't have anything to tie our legs together with and Mrs Parker said no, we couldn't use one of the skipping ropes. So we had to pretend they were tied together – which must have looked very hilarious to anyone who was watching. We couldn't get up a lot of speed like that without our legs doing their own separate thing, but it gave us an idea of what it would be like in the race. I think we're probably going to be a bit limpy. Ryan's not as tall as I am so his legs are shorter than mine and, amazingly, that makes a huge difference.

Still, doing this with Ryan isn't about winning. Winning would be cool but – in the end, if we're limpy, we're limpy.

SATURDAY 20TH JUNE

Homework: None (Mr Mallory away – bad hair joke-free day)
To do: Ring Ryan to see if he can make a three-legged practice in the park today/tomorrow
Mood: Good (hot, though)

10.30am

Sizzling day already. Could be a bit hot for three-legging it later. Might see if Ryan fancies chilling out with an ice cream instead.

Mega mag meeting last night. Everyone's ideas were stonking. Greg said he wanted to use them all but we may not be able to cram everything into the first issue. And everyone really liked my format. Greg thought the book review idea was great.

Paul's big Hot Spot interview's going in too. But it's not going to be an interview with Jesus. Greg said it was an interesting idea but if the magazine got picked up by, say, a non-Christian, it might have a bigger effect on them if they could read an interview with someone whose life had been changed by Jesus. Then he asked me what I thought, as the editor. I mean, wow! My opinion obviously is important in this job! I felt really awkward, though. I didn't want Paul to feel I thought his idea was rubbish – especially as he was so excited about it.

In the end I had to say that maybe Greg was right and someone talking about what it means to have Jesus in your life would probably be a better read. Paul didn't answer.

Greg said, 'It's great you've been thinking about this so much, Paul. It shows you're taking your job seriously, which is exactly what the Hot Spot team needs. So if we discuss ideas and then decide to change them or maybe not to use them, you mustn't be disappointed.'

'I'm not,' Paul said. 'I was just thinking.'

'What were you thinking?' Greg said.

'Can I interview you instead?'

So Greg's going to do the 'Who's On The Hot Spot?' spot. Can't wait to read it, actually.

12.30pm

I was about to ring Ryan, but then the phone went and it was Auntie Janice, so Mum was yabbing away for AGES. Fifty-seven hours later, she called up the stairs that little Jacob was wanting to talk to his big cousin Benny Benny.

I said, 'Jakey! How's it going?'

Jake said, 'I just broke Mummy's best mug.'

I said, 'Oh no. What happened?'

Jake said, 'I was doing drumming like you showed me.'

'Whoops,' I said. (This could be bad for me.) 'Is your mummy cross?'

Jake said, 'No.'

Phew, I thought. 'Well, that's good.'

Jake said, 'I haven't told her.'

'Ah,' I said. 'Maybe it's best to stick to drumming on saucepans. They're stronger than mugs.'

Jake said, 'I <u>was</u> doing drumming on a saucepan but Mummy said, "No, no, no!"'

'So you thought you'd try it on a mug instead?' I asked.

'No,' Jake said. 'When I tried to put the saucepan back, I dropped it on Mummy's mug.'

Fiddlesticks, I thought. Whichever way you look at it, this is probably my fault.

I said, 'Are you worried about telling Mummy?'

'Mmmm,' he said quietly.

I thought, I know I'm going to regret this but I'd better ask anyway. 'Would you like big cousin Benny Benny to tell her for you?'

'Mmmm,' he said again, even more quietly.

'OK,' I sighed. 'Do you want to go and find her?'

He didn't answer but then I heard, very loudly, 'Mummy, Mummy! Benny Benny wants to talk to you!'

Wrong. Benny Benny didn't particularly want to talk to Auntie Janice but I suppose sometimes you just have to do stuff. Incredibly, she was all right about it though. Chatting to Mum must have put her in a good mood. I said please don't be angry with Jake because it was my fault and it only happened because I'd shown him how to drum on saucepans.

She said, 'Don't be silly. Accidents happen. And when Jake's around, they happen quite a lot. Let me go and give him a cuddle.'

I suppose that's one good deed I've done today. It all got me thinking, though. About Ryan. It may be all right to tell someone's mum or dad about something they've done, or something that's happening to them, if they ask you to, but is it all right if they DON'T ask you to? If I find out for definite that Ryan IS being bullied but he still won't talk to anyone about it, should I tell his dad? It's not quite the same thing as dropping a saucepan on a mug.

2.00pm

Mega. Ryan's coming round in about an hour. His dad's dropping him off. I said we could go round the park and practise three-legging it and if we got too hot there was always the ice cream van.

102

Ryan said, 'I don't really want to go to the park.'

I said, 'Why?'

He said, 'I just don't really like it.'

I said, 'Fine. We can practise in the garden.'

He said, 'Cool.'

I said, 'Not really. It's going to be boiling.'

He laughed. Which must be a good sign.

Not too sure about the not liking the park thing, though. EVERYONE likes the park. What's not to like? Except the people who hang around down there which, on a normal Saturday afternoon is more than likely to be the Dixons Gang. And Mickey Martin.

I said to Dad, 'Do you think I should just ask him if he's having a problem with Mickey?'

Dad said, 'No. Not yet. It's too soon. Give him a chance to get to know you a bit first. If there is anything it'd be much better if he felt he could tell you without you having to ask.'

I know that's the right thing to do, I just wish there was a way to speed it up. If I can't help Ryan until he asks me to, it could take forever. And he needs help now, I know he does.

forever!

7.00pm

I think we might be getting it. We must have three-legged it up and down the garden about thirty times. Well, at least twenty, and we were definitely getting faster by the end. If we get a cooler day and we both manage to remember to start with our tied together legs first, I reckon we could be in with a chance in the actual race.

Afterwards we sat up in my room sucking ice cubes.

I said, 'Are you doing any of the other races?'

He said, 'I don't know. I haven't decided yet. I might do the long distance.'

I said, 'I'M doing the long distance.'

He said, 'I know. Dave says you're really good at it.'

I said, 'That's only because I've got long legs. I don't have to go so fast but I can still overtake people.'

Then suddenly he said, 'You've got lots of mates, haven't you?'

'I don't know about lots,' I said, 'but the ones I've got are pretty good. Why? Haven't you?' (I thought that must be an OK question. After all, he brought it up.)

'Dunno,' he said.

Then I saw it – a way to ask him something about Mickey without it being obvious I was trying to find out anything.

I said, REALLY casually, 'What about that new boy, Mickey Martin? Do you get on all right with him?'

Ryan sort of shrugged. I thought he wasn't going to answer but he said, 'He's not really new, is he? He was here before. He's already got mates.'

Then all of a sudden he just stood up. 'I've got to get home. Can your dad drop me back now?'

'Don't you want to finish your ice cubes?' I asked.

'No,' he said. 'You can have them.'

I was right. I could see it. All over his face. He looked like Danny said I used to look when Mickey started on me. Scared. Ryan's in trouble and he thinks he's on his own. The question is,  what do I do about it? ????

SUNDAY 21ST JUNE

Homework: Nil still

To do: Pray for Ryan/Editor's letter

Mood: I want to help Ryan (if you can call that a mood)

9.30am

I've got to keep praying. Dad says if I ask God to open up a way for me to help Ryan, then that's exactly what He'll do. Just please, Lord God, please let it be soon.

3.00pm

Paul screamed up to me at Sunday Club all out of breath and shoved a load of paper into my hand.

He said, 'Saw Greg yesterday. Did the interview. Mum typed it out. That's a copy. You're going to love it. It's ace!'

Just finished reading it. This interview is not ACE. ACE doesn't come anywhere close to what it is. This interview is mega mega MEGA FANSTONKING-TASTICALLY BRILLIANT!

Paul is obviously a genius. I can't believe I never noticed it before. Here's what he's done:

WHO'S ON THE HOT SPOT? ... GREG TAYLER

Paul: So, Greg, what made you want to be a Sunday Club leader?

Greg: I've always liked being around children and young people – I guess I'm just a big kid myself – and I liked the idea of being able to get involved with them in church and share what I know about Jesus.

Paul: A lot of the kids at Sunday Club are quite sporty. Do you have a favourite sport?

Greg: I think that would have to be ice hockey.

Paul: Really? Do you play?

Greg: Not a chance. I have enough trouble standing on my own two feet, let alone trying to race round an ice rink on a couple of blades.

Paul: Is that why you didn't come on the ice-skating trip last Christmas?

Greg: That might have had something to do with it, yes.

Paul: How long have you been a Christian?

Greg: Let me see ... fifteen years and four months. Almost exactly.

Paul: Would you like to tell 'Hot Spot' readers what happened?

Greg: I became a Christian through a church youth club like this one. I'd always believed in God but I suppose I never really thought about it more than that until I started going to this youth club. I used to go sometimes with my brother on a Sunday night. But as we got more involved and started going to Bible studies and listening to what the others were saying, I began to realise that there's a lot more to being a Christian than just believing in God.

Paul: Such as?

Greg: God wants us to be His best friends. He loves us and He wants us to love Him too. But sadly the bad things we do – being selfish, being unkind to each other, getting angry with people, being jealous, taking things that don't belong to us, not telling the truth – all those kinds of things and others as well, which the Bible calls 'sin', get in the way of that friendship with God.

Paul: So what can we do about it?

Greg: What we have to do is actually very simple. But what God did was huge. He loves us so much that He decided to send His only Son, Jesus, into our world to save us from all those bad things that we do. And Jesus did that by dying a very nasty death on a cross for us so that all our sin could be got rid of. His death took it away. And now that's happened, the very simple thing that we have to do is to say that we're sorry for all the bad stuff we've done and ask God to forgive us. Then we can ask Jesus to come into our lives and share them with us and, as soon as we do that and really mean it, that's exactly what Jesus will do. And when you invite Jesus in, you and God can be best friends – forever.

Paul: That's amazing, isn't it?

Greg: It is amazing. Amazing and true.

Paul: And how has being a Christian changed your life?

Greg: Well, for a start, I'm here being interviewed by you.

Paul: That's got to be good then.

Greg: It's better than good. Then there's knowing that God has forgiven me. It's fantastic how I can know I really am friends with Him. I can make the most of my life because I can live it the best way – God's way. We all can. We can talk to Him about anything and everything, whenever we want, and He's always ready to listen and to help us.

Paul: Yes, that is fantastic, but talking to God isn't always easy. There are times when praying is the last thing you feel like doing.

Greg: That's true. Being a Christian doesn't mean that life is always going to be perfect. Things go wrong for Christians just as much as they do for anyone else, and sometimes those are the hardest times to pray. But when you're God's friend, you can know that He wants the very best for you and if you trust Him and talk to Him regularly, He'll be right there beside you, guiding you every day.

Paul: What's the best way to get to know God?

Greg: You can read the Bible. The Bible tells you who God is and what you can do to make Him happy. And you can pray. Praying is all about having a chat. Let's face it, you don't get to know your friends unless you make time for a good natter. It's the same with God. Just natter with Him. He loves it!

Paul: If you could live anywhere in the world, where would it be?

Greg: Right now, you mean?

Paul: Yes.

Greg: Here. Right where I am. Because at the moment, I'm quite sure this is where God wants me to be.

Paul: Do you ever do anything wrong?

Greg: Of course I do! I'm just the same as everyone else. Being a Christian doesn't mean you're perfect. What it does mean is that you must try to live the way God wants and when you do something wrong you need to remember to say sorry. And God will always answer, 'That's OK. Keep trying. Don't give up.'

Paul: Do you have any plans for the future?

Greg: Lots.

Paul: What are they?

Greg: Ah. That would be telling.

Paul: Greg, thank you very much for agreeing to be On The Hot Spot.

Greg: No problem.

I mean sensational, or what? Wow, pressure pressure! My editor's letter is going to have to be really zappy to keep up with that. I was right about wanting to be a rally driver. I think Paul's the one who ought to be the sports journalist – or any kind of journalist, come to that.

3.30pm

Rang Paul.

I said, 'Paul, you star! You're a natural.'

He said, 'A natural what?'

I said, 'A natural interviewer, you teapot!'

He said, 'I knew you'd like it.'

'Like it?' I said. 'I can't get over it.'

He said, 'Greg's pretty good too, isn't he?'

I said, 'Yeah. But YOU asked all the right questions.'

He said, 'Well, you know what I always say.'

'No,' I said.

'If you've got talent,' he said, 'why keep it to yourself?'

Good point.

TUESDAY 23RD JUNE

Homework: Revise for tables test

To do: Try and concentrate on tables and stop thinking about Ryan

Mood: GRUMPY

5.00pm

He won't admit it. Ryan. He just will not admit it. Yesterday he was crying in the toilets again. When I asked him what was wrong he just said, 'Nothing,' and he wouldn't do any three-legged practice at lunchtime. Then today I found him in the cloakroom looking all panicky. The cover was torn off his maths book and he was trying to stick it back on, but the Sellotape had got sort of rucked up and it looked a right mess.

I said, 'What happened to your book?'

He said, 'The cover's come off. What does it look like?'

I said, 'It looks as if it's been ripped off to me.'

He said, 'Yeah, well, it hasn't. It got caught in my bag. This is a brand new book. It's about the third time it's happened. Mrs Parker's going to kill me.'

I said, 'Ryan, is someone messing with your stuff?'

He said, 'No.'

I said, 'Look, if there's a problem, you need to tell someone. Then you can start to sort it out. You can always talk to me, you know.'

He said, 'I haven't got a problem, all right? My book just got caught in my bag.'

'But you said this is the third time it's happened,' I said.

He said, 'Yeah, so?'

I said, 'Fine. Then I think it's about time you got a new bag.'

Why won't he tell me? Doesn't he realise I just want to help?

6.30pm
This is driving me nuts! How can you help someone who won't <u>ask</u> for help?

7.00pm
To be honest, I don't think I can be bothered.

8.15pm
I can't. I really can't.

8.30pm
Mum says I've got to calm down.

She said, 'It can take a lot for someone to admit they're being bullied. When it was happening to you, you didn't tell anyone for a while, did you?'

'I know,' I said, 'but no one knew what was going on so no one really asked the right questions. I DO know what's going on. I could help, but he won't let me. I don't know why I'm bothering.'

Mum said, 'You've got to be patient. Give him more time. Wait till he's ready.'

How are you supposed to be patient over something like this?

9.00pm

Dear Lord, help me to wait for Ryan. I don't want to. I just feel angry. I want him to come out with it. People shouldn't be horrible to each other. People shouldn't make other people feel as if they're worth nothing. It's all wrong. Please sort Ryan out. I don't know if I'm going to be able to now. I really want to, but I just don't know.

9.15pm

Bet I do mega badly in my tables test tomorrow now. Groovy-doovy.

$$7 \times 5 = 35$$
$$8 \times 5 = 40$$
$$9 \times 5 = 45$$
$$10 \times 5 = 50$$

WEDNESDAY 24TH JUNE

Homework: Re-revise tables (Yup, test went really badly – Mr Mallory said maybe I'd be able to think more quickly if my fringe was shorter. Fume fume.)
To do: Boring stuff
Mood: Bored

7.00pm

Hardly been in school five minutes when Alison Filby skipped up to me (yes, she did actually skip) and said, 'Benny, are you going to enter the cover competition?'

I must have looked totally blank (which I was – I didn't have a clue what she was on about, but then I have been a bit busy) because she said, 'You know, the cover competition? To design the cover for the summer holiday issue of "Holly Hill's Own"?'

I blinked (I think).

She said, a bit sniffily, 'Benny, there are posters about it all over school.'

'Oh, THAT competition,' I said, hoping that if I nodded knowingly she wouldn't realise that I hadn't noticed a single poster and didn't really care either.

She said, 'Well? Are you going to give it a go?'

I suddenly realised she was doing it again – giving me one of those smiles where nearly all her teeth showed. I thought, maybe that's how she normally smiles. If it isn't, it's a funny way to show you like someone. Why would you think they want to see your teeth?

'I don't think so,' I said. 'Art's not really my thing.'

'That's silly,' she said. 'I bet your artwork's well cool.'

'Nah. Actually I'm a bit busy at the moment.'

That's when I spotted Paul. He was standing by the notice board with his eyebrows raised. Like Dad's when you mention something like girlfriends or make a comment about his socks. At least I think Paul's eyebrows were raised. Sometimes it's not easy to tell behind his glasses.

I said quickly, 'Anyway, got to go.'

And I went.

Don't say anything, Paul, just don't say a word, I thought. He did, though.

At break he said, 'How's it going with Alison?'

I said (in a bored sort of way – if I sounded annoyed he'd only think I had something to hide), 'How's WHAT going with Alison?'

'You know. IT.'

'There is no IT.'

'You could have fooled me.'

'Yes,' I said, 'well that wouldn't be very hard, would it?'

Sometimes already-made friends are even more irritating than friends you're trying to make.

Which reminds me, ORR is a WOT (waste of time). Ryan's hardly talking to me. I mean, how can you three-leggit with someone who's hardly talking to you? This is the last time I ever get involved in someone else's problems. Ever ever ever.

EVER.

THURSDAY 25TH JUNE

Homework: Draw a plan of your perfect bedroom (Is Mr Mallory a DIY freak, or what?)

To do: ORR: all systems go

Mood: Angry, really ANGRY

4.30pm

He's told me! Finally! Ryan's told me what's going on. Result result result! (Well, not totally, but it's a start.)

Knocked me inside out and back to front, though, I'd never have guessed it. I don't think anyone would. Not even people who are good at guessing things.

It was like this. We had sports day practice this afternoon again. Actual sports day is next week, so we're practising today and tomorrow.

Cool, I thought, no more geography project this week.

I said to Ryan, 'Shall we do some three-legging at lunchtime so we're warmed up for later?'

'No,' he said.

I said, 'Oh, come on. Wouldn't it be so mega if it was you and me blasting first past the finish line?'

He said, 'Look, I don't really want to do it any more. Why don't you find someone else?'

I was crushed. I said, 'It's a bit late for that. Everyone else is already teamed up.'

'It's not <u>my</u> fault,' he said. 'I never wanted to do it in the first place. I wish you'd never asked me.'

I think he was getting ready to cry again.

I said, 'Look, Ryan, are you sure there's nothing going on?'

'No!' he said. 'How many more times?' And he stormed off.

After lunch we all got our PE kit on and went out onto the field. We were sitting down in our groups when I heard Mrs Parker say, 'Where's Ryan?' Everyone was looking around but nobody seemed to know.

Then Mickey put up his hand. 'Shall I go and see if he's still in the cloakroom, Miss?'

No, I thought. Bad idea. Not Mickey.

Mrs Parker started to say, 'Yes, thank you very much, Mickey,' or something like that, but I was already on my feet.

'It's all right, Miss, I'll go,' I said and shot off before she could stop me. Well, I could hardly let Mickey go looking for him, could I?

Ryan was still in the cloakroom. He was sitting on the floor right in the corner. I almost didn't see him.

I said, 'You'd better get out there, Ryan. Mrs Parker's screaming for you.'

He never said a word. Just shook his head.

I said, 'This isn't about the three-legged race, is it? Because if it is, it's cool. I'm not that fussed about doing it anyway.'

He still didn't say anything. I was running out of things to say

116

myself. If only I was Greg, I was thinking. He'd have all the right words and everything.

Then I noticed Ryan had bare feet.

I said, 'Don't you think you ought to get your plims on and go out?'

Not that I honestly expected him to answer. But he did.

'I can't,' he said.

'Why not?'

'They're all wet.'

'How?' I said.

'Doesn't matter.'

'No, Ryan, it does matter.' I had to get him to tell me. 'How did they get all wet?'

He had his head right down now so it was really hard to hear what he was saying.

'They fell.'

'Where?' I said. 'In a puddle?' (Not that there were any puddles. It had been roasting for days.)

He shook his head again. 'Down the toilet.'

'Down the toilet?' I said. 'Ryan, plimsolls don't just fall down the toilet. Did someone put them there?'

Silence.

'Who put them there?' I said again. 'You're in trouble, I know you are. You can't just keep on not telling anyone.'

There was all sorts going on in my head. I was trying really hard not to get annoyed. I was praying like mad. Suddenly I couldn't stop myself.

'Ryan, just tell me! You're not the only one this has happened to. I know exactly what you're going through. Mickey Martin's had it in for me too.'

That's when he looked up at me. Sitting down there in the corner. His face was all kind of pale and pinched.

Then he said it. 'What's Mickey Martin got to do with it?' Huh? Now I really was confused. Ryan was hiding in the corner with his plimsolls soaked in toilet water. He was as white as one of Mum's best lacy pillowcases and he didn't seem to know why it had anything to do with Mickey Martin!

I said, 'It's just … I thought … well, you see … what?' (Sometimes sentences are just too hard to do.)

Ryan said, 'You think this is all Mickey?'

I said, 'Well … yeah … isn't it?'

He shook his head. I think he almost smiled.

I said, 'You don't have to defend him, Ryan, he needs sorting out.'

He said, 'I'm not defending anyone. It's not Mickey. I think it'd almost be easier if it was.'

'Then … who is it?'

No answer. Please, Lord, please help him to tell me.

'You won't believe it,' he said.

'Try me.'

Silence again. Then he put his head back down and mumbled into his knees. But I knew what he'd said as clearly as if he'd spoken the name through a loudspeaker AND written it on a blackboard with flashing lights all around it.

'Alison Filby.'

WHAT? No no no no no. That just wasn't possible.

It wasn't! That couldn't be what he meant.

'Say it again,' I said.

'You heard me the first time.'

Then it all came out. There's a gang of girls picking on him but Alison's the leader. She's been having a bit of a go at him ever since he came to Holly Hill but it's suddenly got a whole lot worse. Ryan thinks it's to do with his dad's job. His dad works with Alison's dad, but a month or so ago, there was a big change around and Alison's dad was made Ryan's dad's boss.

Ever since then she's been so nasty to him. She's been taking his stuff and messing up his books and getting the other girls to do it too. They've been kicking and shoving him. He's got a huge bruise on his leg. I noticed it a couple of days ago but I thought he'd just walked into something. On top of that she's been going round saying how rubbish Ryan's dad is at his job, and how her dad is always saying he wishes he could get rid of him. She even said that if Ryan didn't vote for her to be the school mag editor, she'd get to know about it and then he'd have to pay for being disloyal.

And with all of it, she's told him that if he breathes a word to anyone about what's going on, she'll tell her dad and then Ryan's dad will lose his job just like that.

I sat down beside him. I felt all twisted up inside. It was worse than anything I'd gone through with Mickey, and that was bad enough.

Finally I said, 'It's got to stop. You've got to make it stop.'

He said, 'If I could do that, don't you think I would have done?'

I said, 'You've got to tell your dad.'

'No,' he said. 'I can't tell dad.'

'You've got to. I told my mum and dad about what was going on with Mickey and they came into school and it all got sorted out. The only reason Alison can keep doing this is because you're not telling anyone.'

'No!' he said. 'Dad's got enough problems already. No.'

I said, 'Then talk to Mrs Parker. I'll come with you.'

'No!' he said again. 'I'm not talking to anyone. I shouldn't even be talking to you.'

And that was as far as I could get.

I let Ryan wear my plimsolls so we could go back outside for the rest of sports day practice. They were a bit big but he could still run in them – just a bit sloppily. I was wearing trainers today anyway so I put those back on. Mrs Parker didn't say anything. I told Ryan I'd take his plimsolls home and wash them for him and then his dad wouldn't be wondering what had happened to them.

When we went out to the field, I looked across at Alison and she gave me another one of her teethy smiles. I didn't smile back. I couldn't. I just stared at her. After a minute she looked away, but her smile went all sort of uncomfortable. I saw her say something to the girl sitting next to her. It was one of her 'gang'. Then she looked back at me but she wasn't smiling this time.

8.30pm

Dad was home early for once but Mum said could I not bother him with the Ryan thing this evening because he was tired. She says she's just checked the plimsolls and they're getting dry so they should be all right for tomorrow.

I said, 'I wish Ryan would tell his dad.'

Mum said, 'You can do better than wish. You can pray.'

9.00pm

I know I can pray. And I know God will listen to every word.

But does He answer you if you know you're doing something wrong?

My tummy's still all twisted up. We're not supposed to judge people. God doesn't want us to. He says we all do things wrong so we don't have the right to look down our noses at other people and the bad things they do. I can't help it with Alison, though. How can she do that? How can she make Ryan feel so miserable? She IS worse than Mickey Martin. At least Mickey is what he is. But Alison? All this time she's been pretending to people that she's so goody goody and nice, when underneath, she's really not nice at all.

FRIDAY 26TH JUNE

Homework: Colour in bedroom plan/Tables tables tables (yawn yawn yawn)

To do: Talk to Greg about Ryan

Mood: Needy to talky!

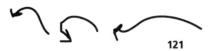

4.30pm

I said to Ryan, 'Is everything OK today?'

He said, 'Yeah. So far.' Then, out of the blue, he suddenly asked, 'Are you one of those churchy people who prays all the time?'

When I'd got over the shock I said, 'I don't know about ALL the time. I mean I'm not praying just now, obviously, because I'm talking to you.'

Ryan said, 'Do you really think it makes a difference?'

I said, 'Yeah. God knows how we feel. He knows everything about us. And He's always got time to listen.'

Ryan said, 'You can't KNOW that.'

I said, 'I do, though. I'm always wittering on to Him.'

He said, 'What, out loud?'

I said, 'Sometimes out loud, sometimes in my head. He hears all of it. I can talk His ear off some days.'

Ryan didn't say anything for a minute, then he asked, 'Have you talked to Him about me?'

I thought, what do I do? Should I tell him or not? But I suppose what would be the point of not telling him?

I said, 'Yeah. Is that all right?'

He just shrugged and that was it. He didn't say anything else.

I can't work it out. I don't know if he's really interested in how it works with God and me or whether he just thinks I'm a freak.

He said later, 'Thanks for ... you know, my plimsolls.'

'No problem,' I said. I suppose if he does think I'm a freak, at least he must be able to see that I'm a helpful sort of freak. Not just a freaky freak.

5.15pm

Dad's home early again but Mum says I need to leave him alone for a bit because he's got some phone calls to make.

I said, 'Can he still drop me down to youth club? I've got to talk to Greg. It's mega urgent.'

She said, 'Is everything all right?'

I said, 'Yeah, yeah, yeah, it's just to do with Ryan, you know.'

Everything's not really all right, but it will be as soon as I've had a chat with Greg.

9.00pm

Not sure about the rally driving thing any more. I mean, it would be really cool and everything and it looks totally wicked when the cars whizz through mud and it whooshes up and slops all over the windscreen, but I'm beginning to think maybe I should be a helping sort of person like Greg. I wonder if you go on courses to learn how to be helpful or if Greg's just naturally ace at it because he's Greg. He always manages to say EXACTLY the right thing.

I said to him, 'If you're really angry with someone but you're praying for something to happen at the same time, does that mean God won't answer your prayers because He wants you to stop being angry first?'

Greg said, 'I think you need to give me a little bit more to go on.'

I told him about Ryan.

I said, 'I've been asking God to help him find a way to tell his dad. The trouble is my insides have all gone manic. I can't get rid of all my bad feelings. I'm so angry with the girl whose been doing the bullying. It's just not fair.'

'You're right, it ISN'T fair,' Greg said, 'and I expect it feels even more unfair to you because you know what it's like to be bullied.'

I said, 'But when Mickey Martin was bullying me, I wasn't angry with him. I didn't even not like him. I just wanted it all to stop. It's different with this girl. She's wrecking Ryan's life – and she's getting such a kick out of doing it. I mean, he's never done anything to her. Why doesn't she just leave him alone? I know I shouldn't but … I really think I hate her.'

This is what I mean about Greg. If I'd said 'I hate her' to anyone else (Mr Mallory, for example), they'd have probably said something like, 'Come on now, you know it's not very nice to hate people,' or '"Hate" is a bit of a strong word, isn't it, Benny?'

Greg didn't. He said, 'You've got every right to be angry. It's a good thing in a way. It shows how much you care. I bet God's angry too. And sad. But the thing about God is that He doesn't want us to hate anybody. No matter what they've done. God never hates us. He loves us and He doesn't stop loving us. What He hates is the horrible things we do, and you need to try and do that too. You can hate what this girl is <u>doing</u>, but you have to try not to hate <u>her</u>.'

'How?' I said. 'How do you separate someone from the things they do?'

'Practice, I suppose,' Greg said. 'God does it. Every day. He's doing it for you right now.'

I said, 'But it's easy for Him. He's God, isn't He?'

Greg said, 'I don't think it's easy for Him at all. I think what makes it possible is the fact that He loves us so much. It's hard for us even to begin to understand just how massive His love for everyone is. Keep praying for

Ryan. You're right, he does need to talk to his dad as soon as possible. And there's something else you can do too.'

'What's that?' I said. I was thinking, please don't tell me I've got to pray for Alison.

He didn't.

He said, 'You can ask God to help you forgive the bully.'

You see? He's brilliant. I'd never have thought of that.

9.50pm

Greg's still brilliant but do you think he has any idea how hard it is to ask God to help you forgive someone you don't want to forgive? I've been sitting here for half an hour and nothing's coming out.

10.10pm

Rang Greg.

Mum said, 'You can't bother him at this time of night.'

I said, 'I've got to. He won't mind. I was talking to him before.'

She gave me one of her 'the things you get away with, young man' looks and went back to sit with Dad.

I said to Greg, 'I don't think I can do it. I don't think I can ask God to help me forgive her. It's too hard.'

Greg said, 'It is hard, but you know what? Jesus DIED so that God could forgive you. How hard do you think that was?'

10.30pm

I'm sorry, Lord, I'm sorry I'm so angry.
Please forgive Alison for what she's
doing to Ryan. And somehow help
me to forgive her too. Amen.

SATURDAY 27TH JUNE

Homework: None
To do: Finish editor's letter
Mood: OK (no, actually, could be a lot better)

10.00am

Sometimes parents can be so weird. You know exactly
where you are with them for years because they do
the same old stuff (except sometimes when your dad
decides he's going to start embarrassing you by playing
the bass guitar in front of people, or your mum goes
and buys a mountain bike because keeping fit 'doesn't
just happen by itself, you know'). Then suddenly they
do something that is just so UN-them that you realise
you don't know where you are with them at all.

I reminded God that Ryan really needed His help at
the moment (I've got to keep asking for him because
I'm pretty sure he's not going to ask for himself yet),
then I went down to have breakfast. No Dad. There's
ALWAYS Dad at breakfast on a Saturday morning. It's
just one of those things that always is – like walking into
the lounge and there's the sofa.

I said to Mum, 'Where's Dad?'

Mum said, 'He just fancied a walk.'

A walk? First thing on a Saturday morning? I don't
think so.

'Why?' I said.

'He just felt like it, Benny. How many pieces of toast would you like?'

You see what I mean? Dad doesn't do that. He just doesn't. I mean, it's not as if we've got a dog or anything.

11.00am

Dad's still not back from his 'walk'. I asked Mum if she thought he might have fallen down a hole or something but she said that, just because people sometimes need a bit of peace and quiet, it doesn't mean they've fallen down a hole.

That's the other thing about parents. They have no sense of humour.

11.30am

STILL no dad. What is going on here? Doesn't he realise I have to try and finish my editor's letter this weekend because Greg wants to try and get everything together by next Friday so we can get the first 'Hot Spot' out? How does he expect me to concentrate when he's stuck down a hole somewhere?

I asked Mum if I could ring a few people to see how they were getting on with their mag bits and she said, 'Couldn't you have talked to them last night? All these phone calls cost money, you know.'

I said, 'I didn't have time to talk to anyone last night. I was having a very important conversation with Greg.'

She said, 'All right, but please try and be quick.'

I've got editor's responsibilities to sort out and I'm being told I've got to be quick on the phone. How unreasonable is that?

12.05pm

Dad's back. He's having a cup of coffee in the kitchen with Mum. I asked him if he'd had a nice walk and he just said, 'Yeah, thanks. What are you up to?'

I told him I was trying to finish my editor's letter.

Silence.

I said, 'You can read it later if you want.'

He said, 'Thanks. I will do.'

More silence.

I said, 'It's good that Ryan talked to me, isn't it? Now he's told someone, maybe he'll find it easier to tell his dad.'

Dad said, 'Let's hope so. You're doing a great job, Benny.'

And that was it. That was as much of a conversation as I could get out of him.

I asked Mum if I could have a milkshake.

She said, 'Of course you can. I'll bring you one up in a minute.'

She'll bring me one UP? It's obvious, then. They don't want me sitting in the kitchen with them. They want to have one of their private, grown-up 'chats'. Without me.

I don't understand. It's Saturday. Saturdays are fun. What's happened to this one?

2.15pm

UNBELIEVABLE. Dad's gone out again. He hasn't taken the car. He must be using up a whole year's worth of walking in one day.

I said to Mum, 'What is it? Some kind of keep fit thing? Can I go and watch?'

She said, 'Leave him alone. He's just popped round to see Martin.'

What? He NEVER goes round to see Martin. Not in the middle of a Saturday afternoon. Anyway, it's church tomorrow. He could see him there. Martin IS our church minister. It's not as if he'll have decided to go windsurfing instead of turning up, is it?

It's all weird today. Weird, weird and weirder.

3.30pm

John rang. He said he'd just finished working out fifteen questions for the Bible quiz and was that enough? I said I was sure it was plenty and to bring them along to Sunday Club tomorrow because Greg wants the mag out before the summer break.

Everyone's going to have their stuff in before me. I've got to finish this letter.

Parents can be so selfish sometimes.

4.00pm

I've started thinking. (Not always a good thing.) Dad was home early from work on Thursday and Friday. Mum's been saying I need to leave him alone because he's tired. Now he's disappearing off on his own and popping out for chats with Martin.

I know what it is. He's ill. He must be. He must have

something really bad wrong with him but he doesn't want to tell me so I won't worry.

Well, too late, I AM worried. I'm a sensitive, almost mature person. Of course I'm going to worry when my dad starts going out for walks for no apparent reason.

6.00pm

Dad was watching TV and Mum was on her own in the kitchen.

I said really quietly, 'What's wrong with Dad? Is he ill?'

Mum said, 'Why ever would you think that?'

I said, 'You're not telling me today's been normal.'

She said, 'Dad's not ill. It's nothing like that.'

I said, 'So what is it, then?'

She said, 'Sit down there a minute. Let me go and get him. I knew we should have told you. I said you'd be bound to notice something was up.'

When Dad came in he said he was sorry if he'd worried me and he was fine. No doctor needed. He said he hadn't told me anything because he hoped he could sort things out a bit first. Anyway, they were his problems. His and Mum's. I wasn't to get bothered by them.

I said, 'How can I not be bothered when I know something's wrong?'

Then he told me.

He's losing his job.

9.00pm

I don't think I ever want to be a grown-up. So much of what goes on in their world is crazy. Apparently someone can be really good at their job but still be asked to leave because suddenly the boss doesn't want so many people working for him.

craz4

Dad says it's just life. I say it's just rubbish. TREBLE dustbins full.

SUNDAY 28TH JUNE

Homework: As Saturday (ie none)
To do: Pray lots for Dad
Mood: Better since Sunday Club

2.00pm

Greg said we'd start Sunday Club off a bit differently this week. He said he wanted us to do some serious praying because he'd been hearing some very sad stories lately and he thought it would be a good idea if we all talked to God about them together. So if there was someone in particular we wanted God to help, then now was a good time to ask Him. He said we didn't have to pray out loud if we didn't want to. The important thing was to ask God to be with anyone we know who's in trouble.

He was talking about Ryan, I know he was. At least, that had to be one of the sad stories he'd heard. I wondered if he knew about Dad. After all, Dad had been to see Martin, and Greg and Martin must talk all the time.

Then Greg started telling us lots of other stuff. Got to write this all down because it was really mega.

Greg said, 'Becoming a Christian not only means making friends with God, it also means becoming part of His huge family. Now, the family of God is sort of like your own body. Your body's got a head – which is the most important part because that's where your brain is, and it's your brain that guides the rest of your body so it knows what to do – and then it's got all sorts of other bits and pieces to help you live your life.

'You've got your hands and fingers for stuff like eating and putting on your make-up. Then you've got your legs and feet for walking around and kicking footballs. You've got your tongue for melting chocolate on, your nose for blowing when you've got a cold, and on and on. You know what I'm saying.

'But just think about it,' he went on, 'if you've got a sore finger or a sore toe or your tummy aches or your ears hurt, it makes you feel not well, doesn't it? One part of your body doesn't feel right, even a very small part, and suddenly the whole of the rest of you just feels off. So what do you do? You do what you can to help the sore bit get better.

'That's what it's like with God's family. We belong to each other. We're all one "Body", in just the same way as the different bits and pieces of our separate bodies fit together to make up a whole person. And God is the Head who guides us through our lives and helps us know what to do. But when one part of the Body is sore – when one of the family members is hurting – the rest of the Body doesn't feel so good. That's when you need to pray for that person, that God will help them feel better, that He'll help them through whatever it is that's making them ill or sad.

'We're not supposed to struggle on by ourselves. We've got God and we've got each other, and when we share with each other and pray for each other, we're building up His family – just like it says in the Bible.' (Good or what?)

John said, 'What about people who aren't in God's family? People who aren't Christians? We need to pray for them when they feel sad too, don't we?'

'Of course we do,' said Greg. 'God loves all of us, whether we've made friends with Him yet or not. And when we pray for people altogether, like we're going to do in a moment, then God knows we're really serious about what we're saying, and it makes our prayers even stronger.'

Sometimes you don't really think about whether it's right to mention something or not, you just come out with it. It was like that this morning. I couldn't help it.

I didn't think, I just said, 'Can I say something?'

Greg said, 'Go ahead.'

Everyone was looking at me. (I suppose they would be. If I'd been sitting there and someone had said, 'Can I say something?' like that, I'd be looking at them.) I knew I was going bright red. It was too late now, though, I had to say it.

I said, 'It's about my dad. I know everyone's probably got someone else who needs praying for. I've got someone else too. Apart from my dad, I mean. He's someone who's not God's friend at the moment, but I think he might be one day because he's been asking me some funny questions. But my dad really needs praying for today, too, and I don't suppose you'd think about praying for him unless you knew something was wrong.'

Then I told them. Dad was losing his job and he didn't know what he was going to do. It was horrible. I thought I was going to cry. I mean, I NEVER cry. Well, only sometimes. It's just that he's my dad. And I really love him.

Greg said I'd been brave. I don't know why, I don't feel brave. He said lots of us are afraid to talk about things that are wrong. Either we're too embarrassed, or we think we should always be able to sort everything out by ourselves. Or perhaps we don't trust other members of God's family enough to talk to them. We can discuss other people's problems but we keep our own to ourselves. He said that, by talking about what had happened to Dad, I showed that I trusted the people around me. And I was living in the way God wanted me to by sharing with His family and asking them to help pray for another part of the Body.

Then he said, 'Phew! After all that, I think we deserve a Quality Street. Then we'll pray.' And he went and grabbed one of those massive tins from behind his desk.

Greg is just **SO COOL!** What a fanstonkingtastic job, though – always knowing the right thing to say and being able to help people. I really do need to think about this.

I said to Dad when we got home, 'I reckon you could do a job like Greg. You quite often know the right thing to say.'

Dad did the raising his eyebrows face. 'Only "quite often"?' he said.

'Well, you could probably learn how to get it right all the time,' I said. 'Greg could teach you.' (The bass guitar thing worries me slightly, but I didn't think this was the time to be negative.)

4.30pm

My Dad is so great. He's got huge problems but he's still been down the park playing footie with John and me.

I said to him, 'You don't seem so worried today or are you just pretending?'

He said, 'Oh no, I am worried. It's just that, when I went round to see Martin yesterday, we prayed for quite a long time. Then in church this morning, I suddenly remembered something I'd said to you when you didn't get the school magazine job and Greg asked you to take on the one for Sunday Club.'

I knew what he was going to say.

I said, 'You told me that something can seem like the end of the world, but then it turns out not to be because God's got a much better thing waiting for you.'

'Amazing,' Dad said. 'And there was me thinking you never listen to a word I say.'

I said, 'Do you think God's going to find you a better job?'

'I don't know,' he said, 'but what I DO know is that He's always there. Sometimes it feels as though He's a long way away, but that's just to do with how we might be feeling, and not to do with where God is. God doesn't go away. So, things might be hard for a while but we have to try and trust Him and keep on talking to Him. I don't know what's going to happen, but He's always looked after us so far, hasn't He?'

Come to think of it, Dad does know the right thing to say most of the time.

Nearly all of the time actually.

Definitely.

Top Sunday.

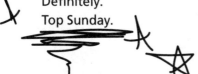

MONDAY 29TH JUNE

Homework: English sheet
To do: Pray for Dad and Ryan
Mood: So so (which isn't bad considering all the stuff that's going on)

4.30pm

No Ryan today. I was looking everywhere for him, then I saw Dave and he said he wasn't in. What does that mean? Did he stay off because he thinks I'm going to keep on at him to tell his dad about what's happening? Is he hiding from Alison? Maybe his dad thinks he's at school but actually he's bunked off somewhere? He could be lying in a ditch with a broken leg.

Or I suppose he could just have a sore throat or something.

Have you ever noticed how not knowing something that might be really bad is so much worse than knowing something for definite that IS really bad? (Well, I know what I mean.)

5.00pm

Greg rang. He said he knows things aren't exactly easy at the moment, but if I could get my editor's letter finished for Friday, then we could meet up over the weekend and put all the other bits and pieces together ready to get the 'Hot Spot' printed and out for a proper launch party at youth club on Friday 14th July.

'I thought we could have a barbecue,' he said, 'and I promise you I won't do the cooking.' (That's a relief. If there's one thing Greg can't do, it's sausages.)

9.00pm

If anyone else apart from me was inside my life right now, never in a million, billion, trillion, zillion, and whatever comes after that, years could they say being a Christian is boring.

Sometimes things just go on and on without much changing, but then you suddenly get hit by this real rollercoaster of stuff and it's one thing after the other. If I wasn't so happy (not to mention amazed, knocked out, flabbergasted, gob-smacked, etc, etc), I'd probably be exhausted. When God starts to work something out, He doesn't hang about!

At 7 o'clock the doorbell went.

Mum said, 'Who on earth is that? I'm just about to put the food out.'

'I'll go,' Dad said.

Mum said, 'Whoever it is, can you tell them we're just about to eat?'

I heard Dad open the door. After a few minutes he called upstairs, 'Benny, someone to see you.'

Mum said, 'Please don't be long. It'll get cold.'

Dad said, 'You might want to pop it in the oven.'

Mum hates that. Having to keep food warm after she's cooked it. (The strangest things can put her in a bad mood.)

I got to the bottom of the stairs. Mum was standing in the kitchen doorway. Dad was by the front door.

Then I saw them. Ryan first, but not just Ryan. Ryan and his dad.

I looked at MY dad. What was this? It was one of those 'have I done something horribly wrong without realising it?' moments.

Ryan said, 'All right, Benny?'

I said, 'Yeah. You?'

He nodded.

Dad said, 'Look, why don't we go in the lounge and sit down?'

Ryan's dad said, 'What about your meal? We don't want to disturb you. We just wanted a quick word.'

Dad looked at Mum and said, 'It can wait for a bit.'

Mum said, 'Of course it can. Go on through.'

If my mouth had dropped open any wider I think my tongue would have fallen out.

We sat down and Mum went to put the kettle on.

Ryan's dad said, 'Sorry to just barge in, but … we wanted to come round and say thank you, Benny. Well, especially me. I wanted to say thank you.'

It must be the plimsolls, I thought. Ryan must have told him I'd washed them.

Ryan's dad said, 'I've known for a while there's been something wrong with Ryan. I didn't know what it was, though. And I've been so busy with work, I suppose I haven't really tried to find out. I hoped it was just one of those phase things that would go away on its own.'

I still wasn't sure exactly where this was going.

'Anyway,' he went on, 'the point is, Benny, it turns out you were looking after him better than I was. You knew someone was causing trouble for him and you managed to get him to talk to you about it.'

My heart was thumping in my ears. I wish it wouldn't do that.

'And because he opened up to you,' he said, 'he finally opened up to me. Last night. Late last night. Which is why I thought we both deserved a day off today.'

I looked at Dad. He was smiling. I was smiling myself. My face must have looked more like a big smile than face actually.

Dad said, 'Have you decided what you're going to do?'

Ryan's dad said, 'I've already spoken to the head teacher. I'm going into school with Ryan in the morning and we're going to have a meeting with him. What I'd like to do if possible is to get this all sorted out without involving Alison's dad.'

'Is that because you think you'll lose your job?' I asked.

'No, Alison's dad and I get on pretty well. I just don't think there's going to be the need to tell him. What Alison's counting on is that Ryan won't give her away. Now that he has and she's going to have to stand up in front of not just the head teacher, but me as well, and admit to what she's doing, I'm hoping it'll stop.'

'And if it doesn't?' Dad said.

'If it doesn't then I WILL go and talk to her dad. But somehow I don't think Alison's going to be too keen on that.'

Then we all had a cup of tea. Well, Mum and the two dads had a cup of tea, like they do. Ryan and I had strawberry milkshakes. Mum even put ice cream in the top.

9.40pm

I said to Dad, 'Do you think Ryan's going to be all right now?'

Dad said, 'There's probably a bit of a way to go yet. Apart from anything else, Alison Filby is going to have to face up to herself, which isn't going to be easy for her.'

'It's a good start, though, isn't it?' I said.

'It's a fantastic start.'

He went to the window and was about to draw the curtains when he suddenly looked back over at me.

'I'm really proud of you, Benny boy. You're not half bad, you know that?'

I said, 'Can you leave the curtains a minute? I just want to write that down!'

IF YOU LIKED THIS BOOK, YOU'LL LOVE THESE:

TOPZ

An exciting, day-by-day look at the Bible for children aged from 7 to 11. As well as simple prayers and Bible readings every day, each issue includes word games, puzzles, cartoons and contributions from readers. Fun and colourful, *Topz* helps children get to know God.
ISSN: 0967-1307
£2.25 each (bimonthly)
£12.50 UK annual subscription (6 issues)

TOPZ FOR NEW CHRISTIANS

Thirty days of Bible notes to help 7- to 11-year-olds find faith in Jesus and have fun exploring their new life with Him.
ISBN-13: 978-1-85345-104-1
ISBN-10: 1-85345-104-5
£2.49

TOPZ GUIDE TO THE BIBLE

A guide offering exciting and stimulating ways for 7- to 11- year-olds to become familiar with God's Word. With a blend of colourful illustrations, cartoons and lively writing, this is the perfect way to encourage children to get to know their Bibles.
ISBN-13: 978-1-85345-313-7
ISBN-10: 1-85345-313-7
£2.49